LEGO NINJAGO
Masters of Spinjitzu

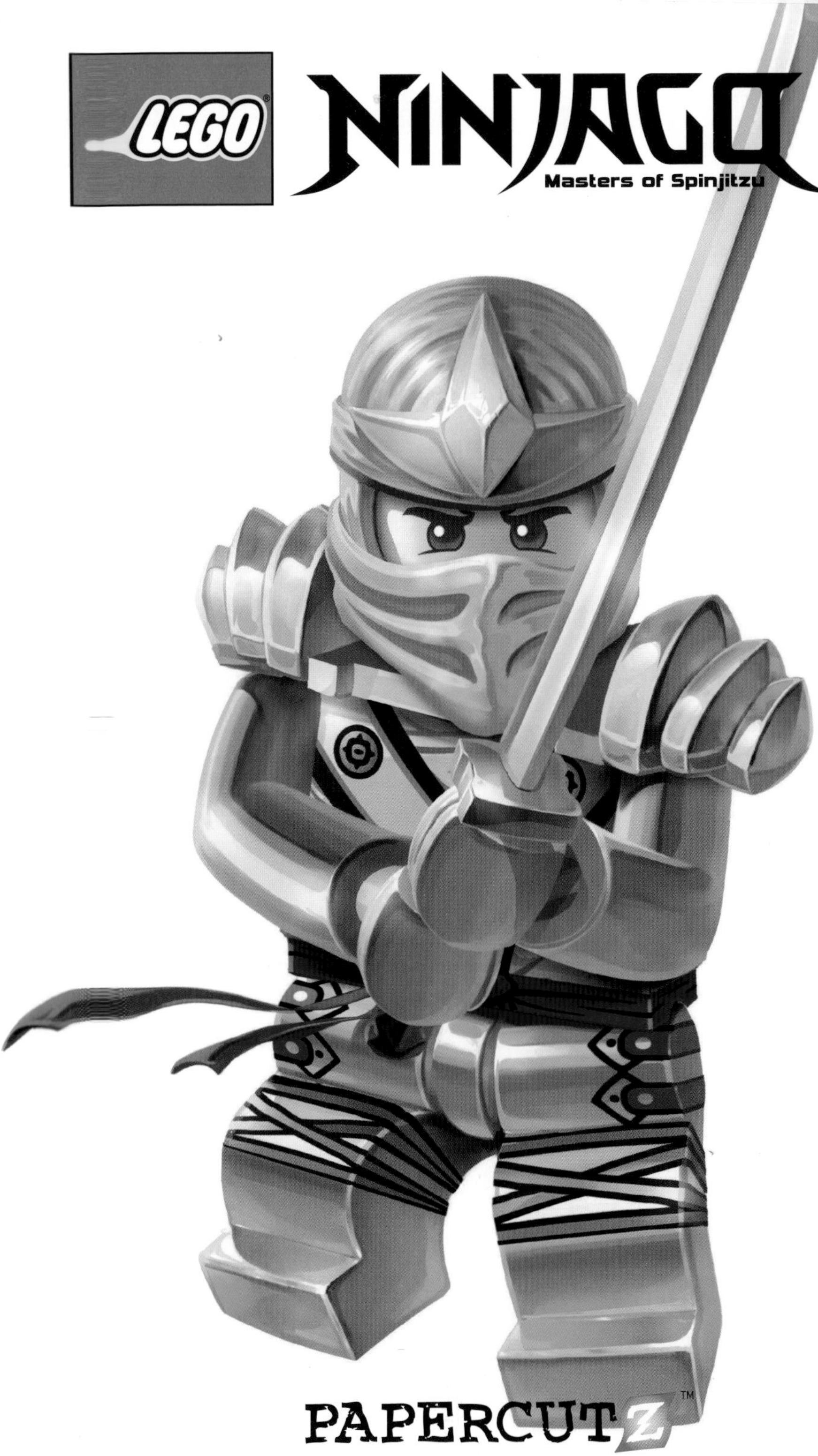

PAPERCUTZ™

LEGO NINJAGO

Masters of Spinjitzu

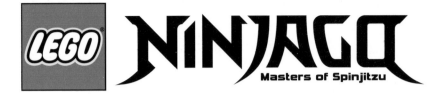

"WARRIORS OF STONE"

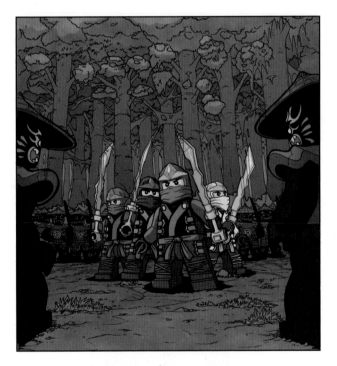

Greg Farshtey – Writer

Jolyon Yates – Artist

Jayjay Jackson – Colorist

Paulo Henrique – Cover Artist

Laurie E. Smith – Cover Colorist

PAPERCUTZ

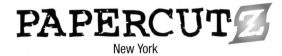

New York

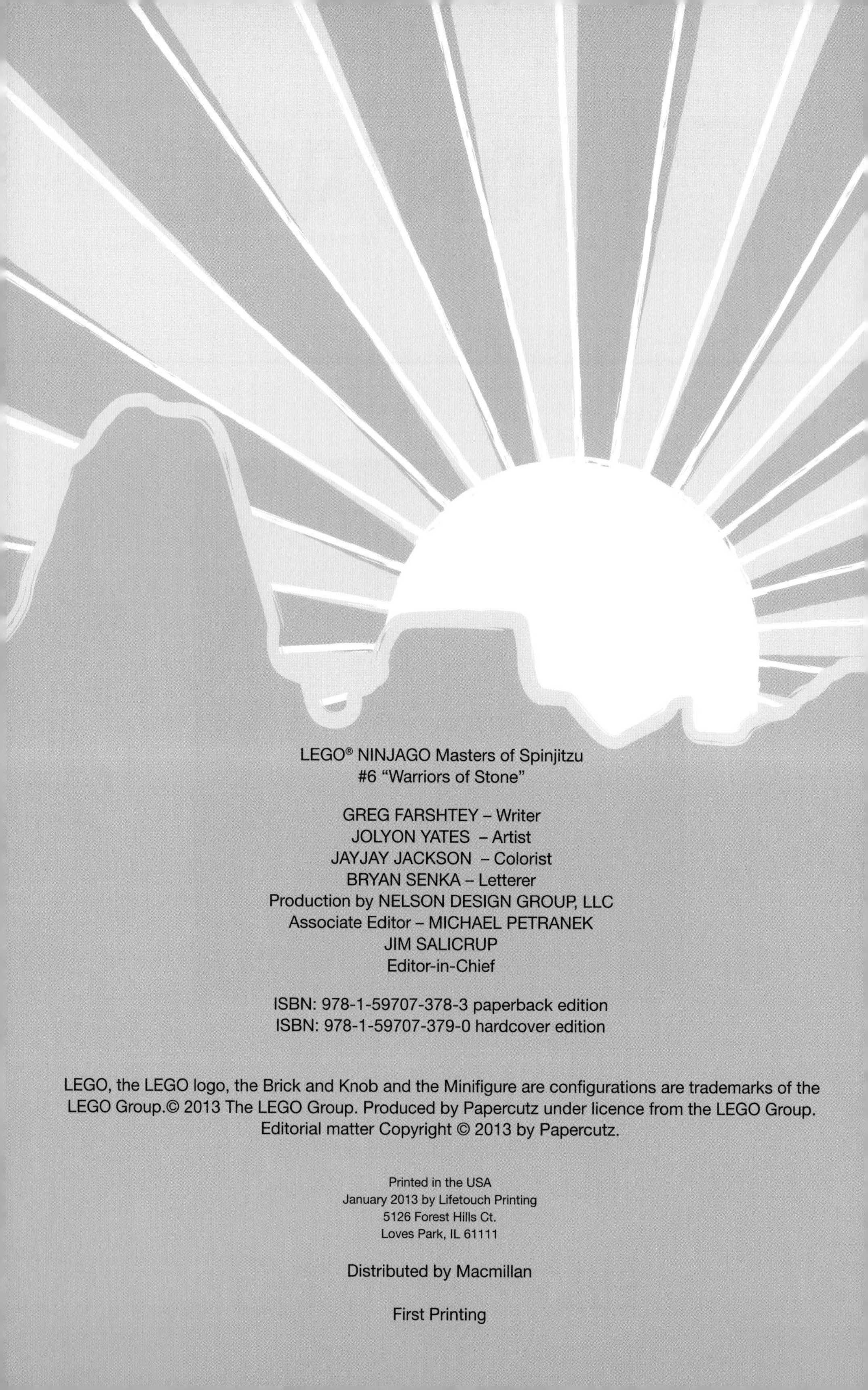

LEGO® NINJAGO Masters of Spinjitzu
#6 "Warriors of Stone"

GREG FARSHTEY – Writer
JOLYON YATES – Artist
JAYJAY JACKSON – Colorist
BRYAN SENKA – Letterer
Production by NELSON DESIGN GROUP, LLC
Associate Editor – MICHAEL PETRANEK
JIM SALICRUP
Editor-in-Chief

ISBN: 978-1-59707-378-3 paperback edition
ISBN: 978-1-59707-379-0 hardcover edition

Printed in the USA
January 2013 by Lifetouch Printing
5126 Forest Hills Ct.
Loves Park, IL 61111

Distributed by Macmillan

First Printing

MEET THE MASTERS OF SPINJITZU...

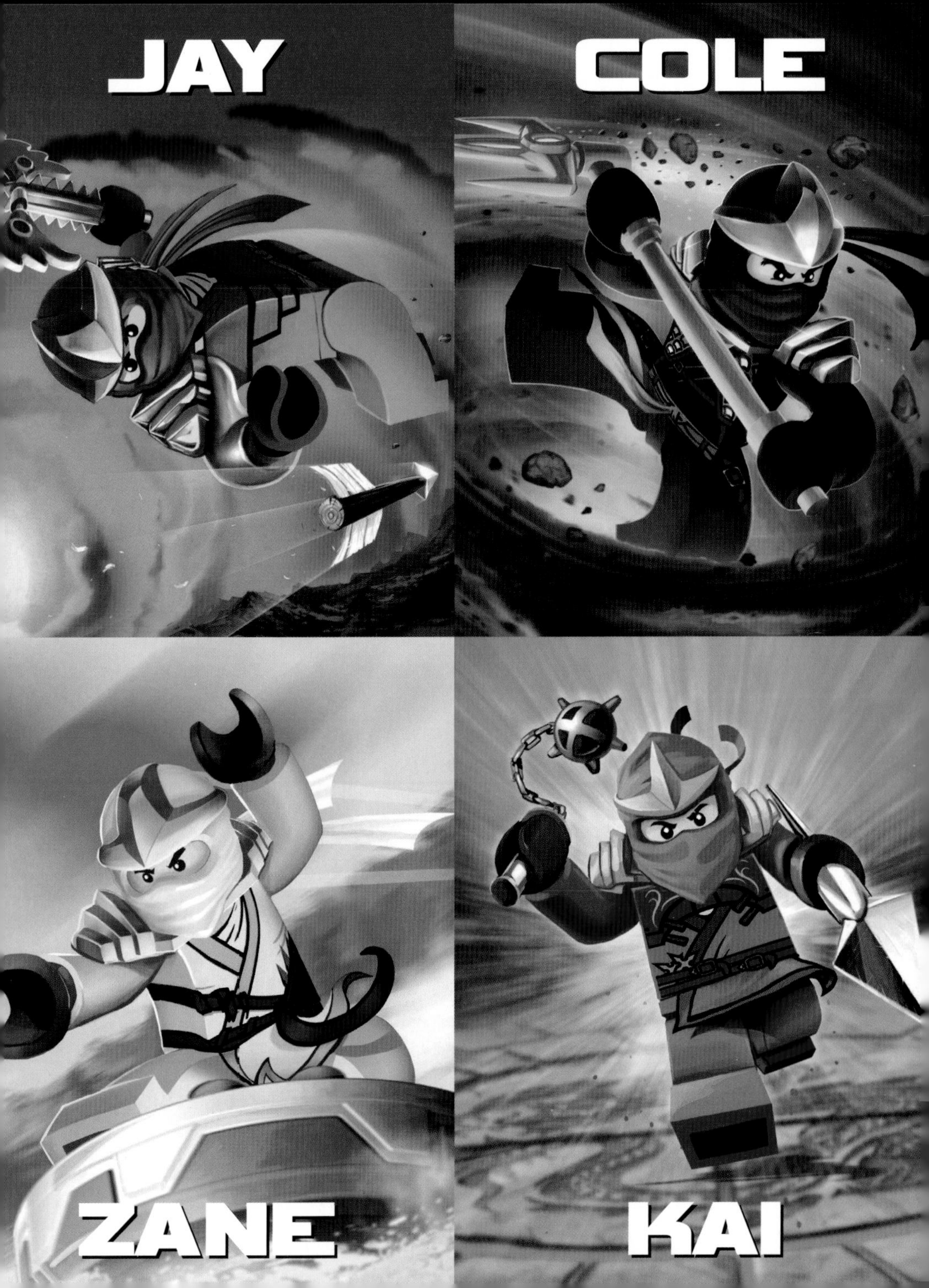
JAY
COLE
ZANE
KAI

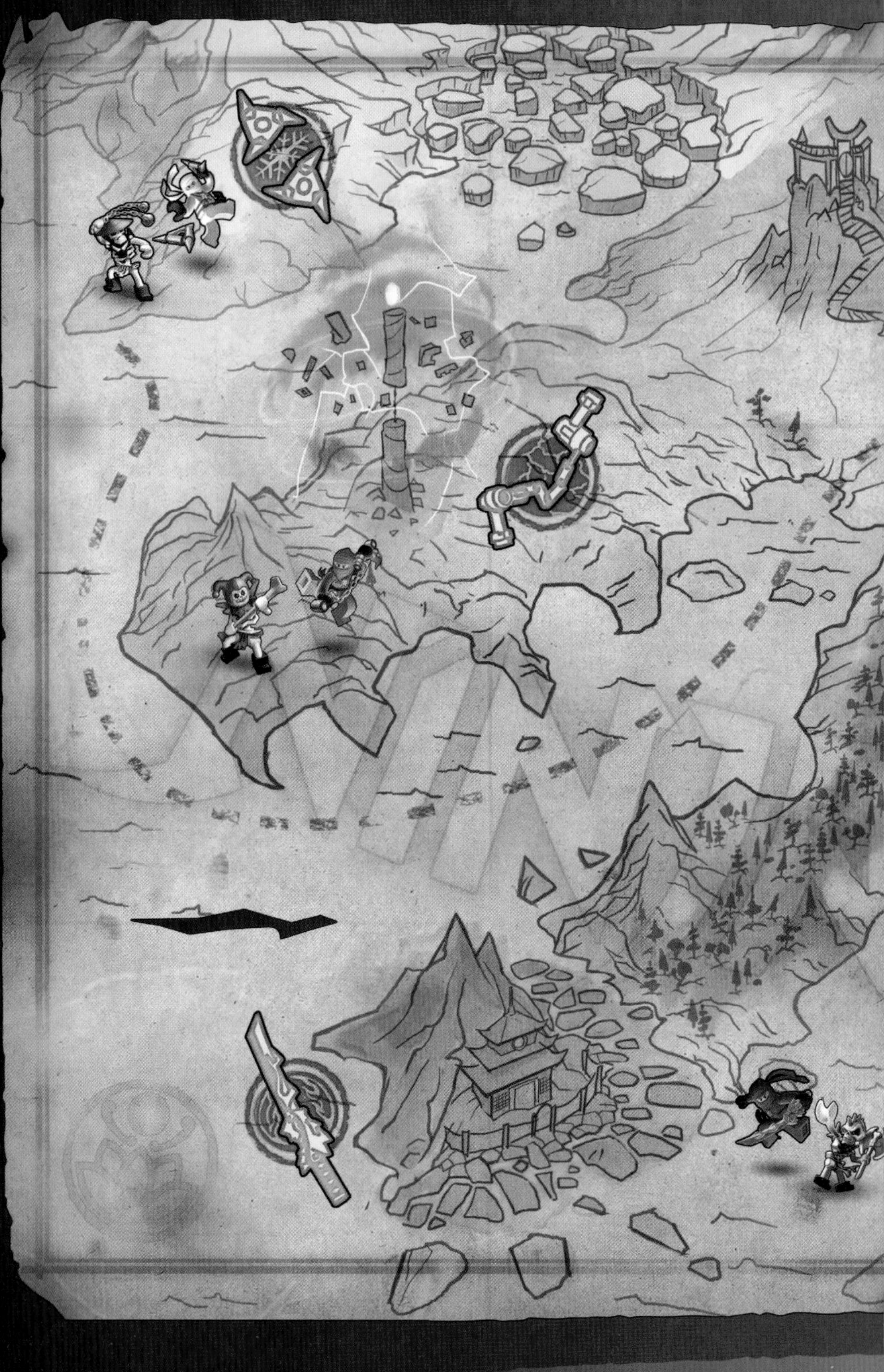

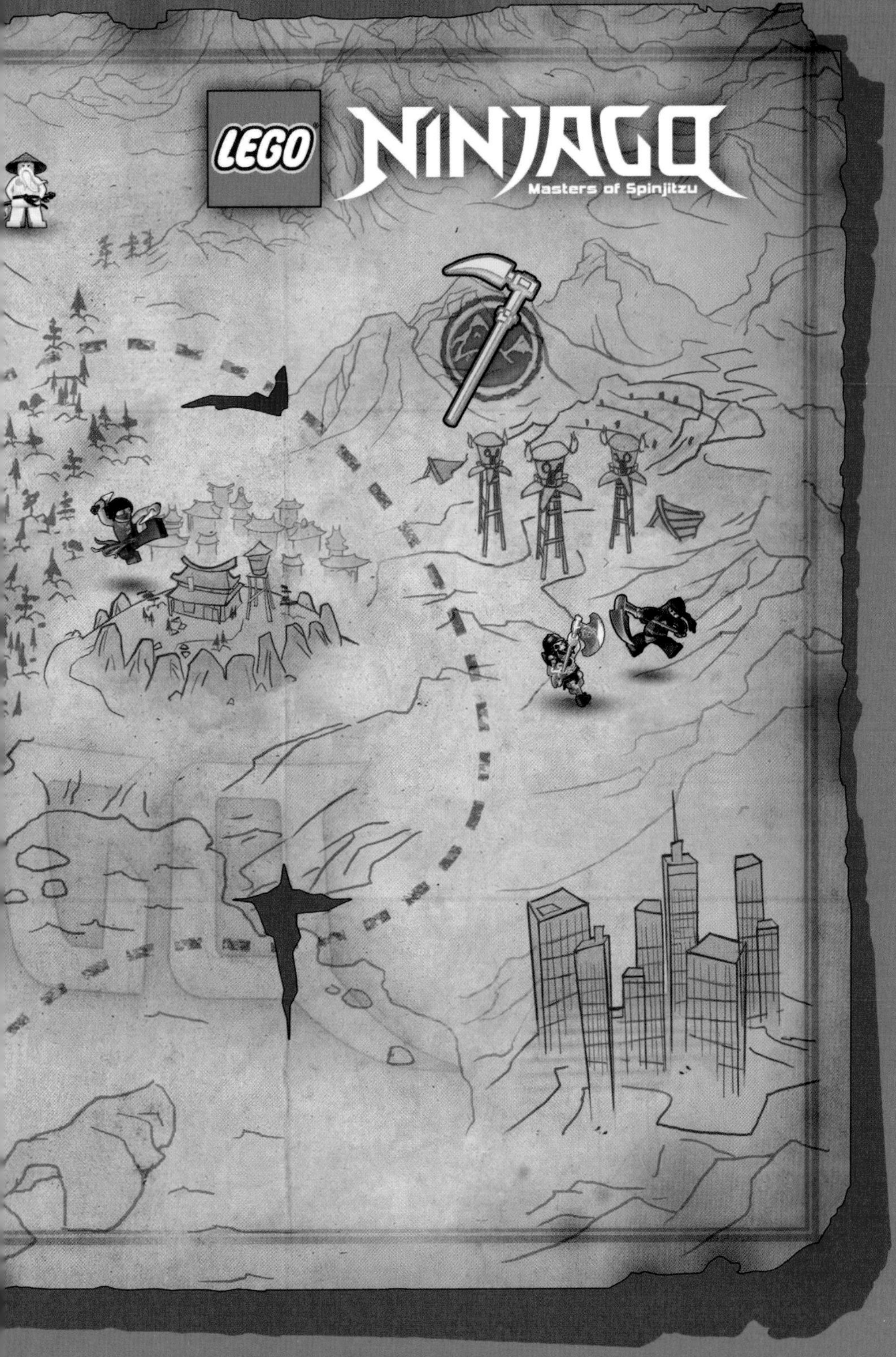
LEGO
NINJAGO
Masters of Spinjitzu

And the Master of the Masters of Spinjitzu...

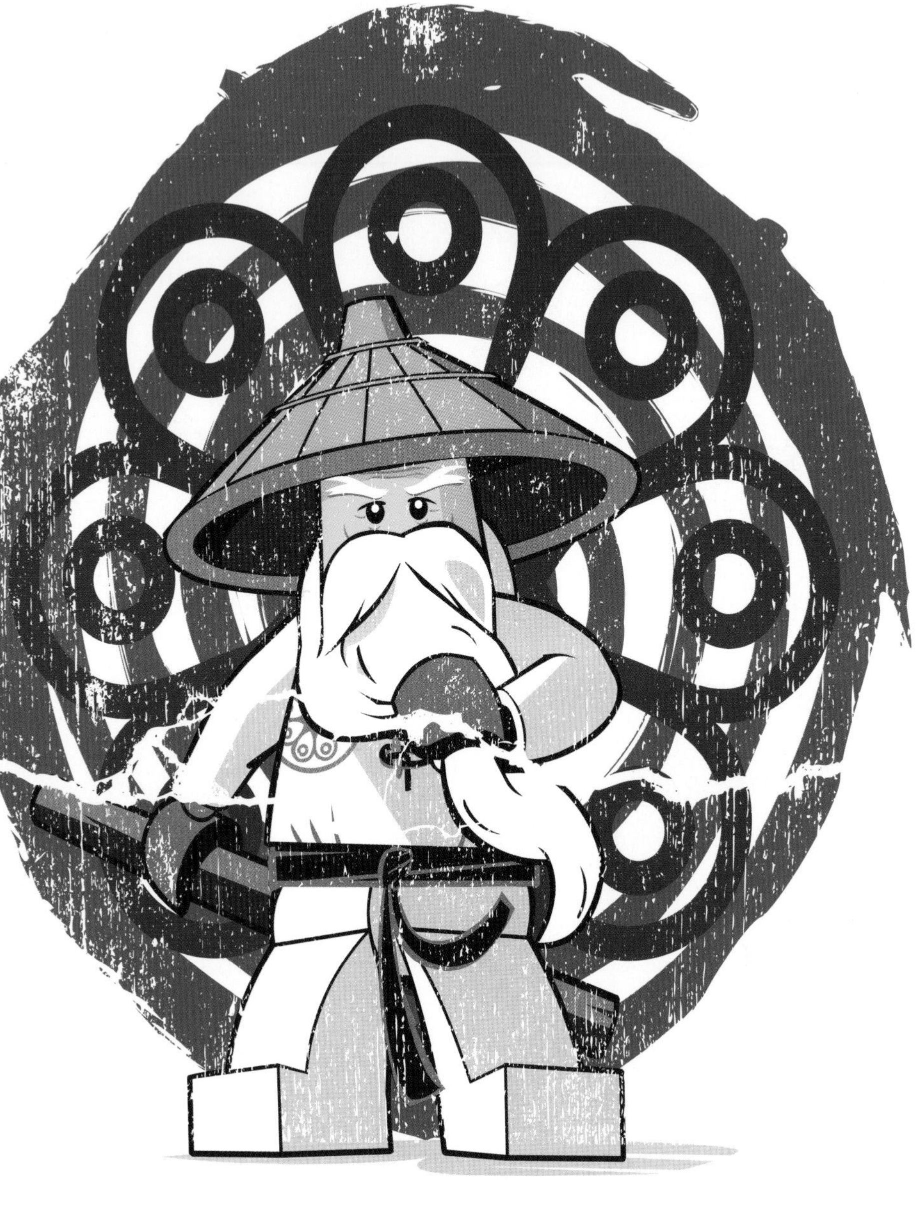

SENSEI WU

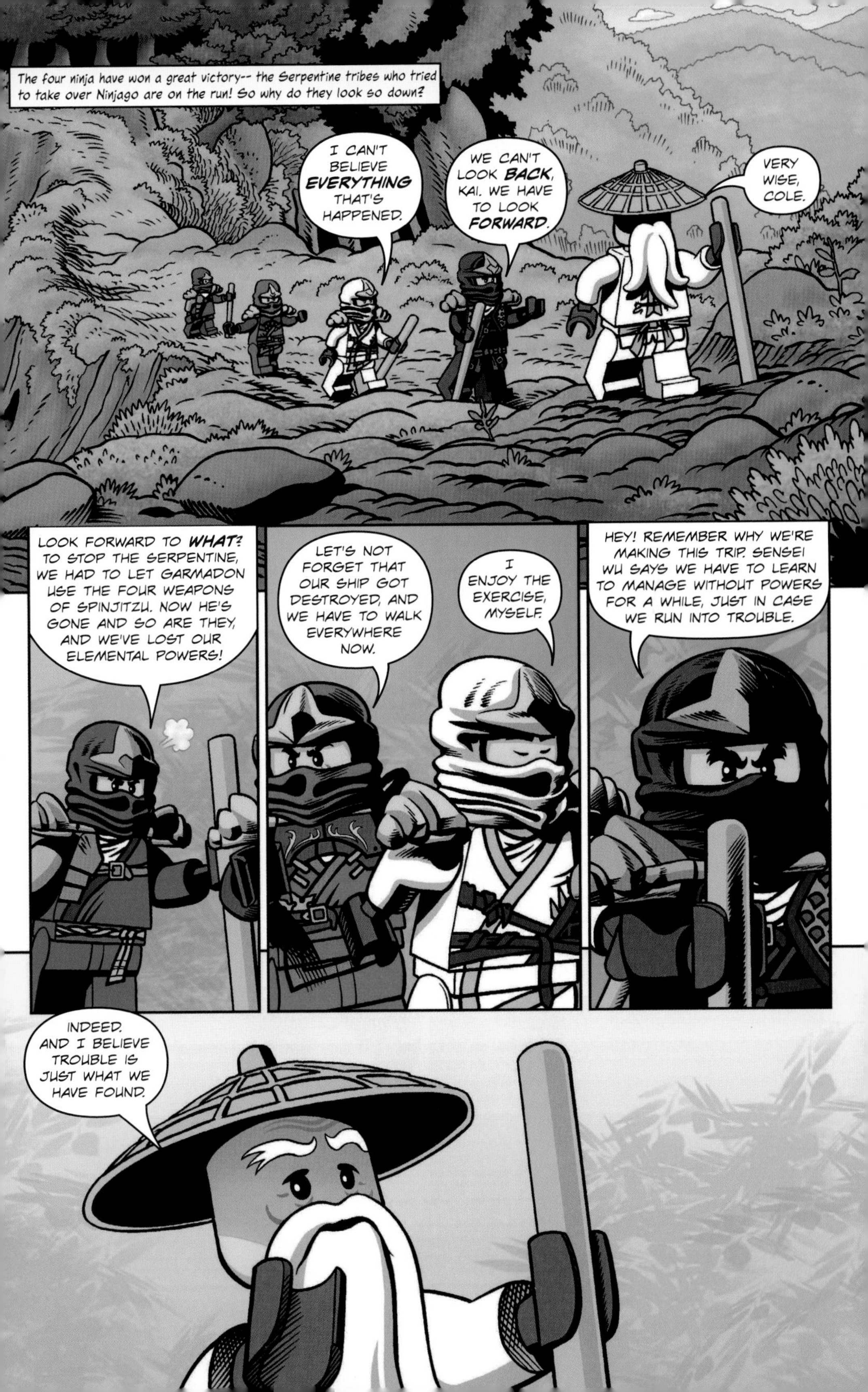

The four ninja have won a great victory-- the Serpentine tribes who tried to take over Ninjago are on the run! So why do they look so down?
I CAN'T BELIEVE EVERYTHING THAT'S HAPPENED.
WE CAN'T LOOK BACK, KAI. WE HAVE TO LOOK FORWARD.
VERY WISE, COLE.
LOOK FORWARD TO WHAT? TO STOP THE SERPENTINE, WE HAD TO LET GARMADON USE THE FOUR WEAPONS OF SPINJITZU. NOW HE'S GONE AND SO ARE THEY, AND WE'VE LOST OUR ELEMENTAL POWERS!
LET'S NOT FORGET THAT OUR SHIP GOT DESTROYED, AND WE HAVE TO WALK EVERYWHERE NOW.
I ENJOY THE EXERCISE, MYSELF.
HEY! REMEMBER WHY WE'RE MAKING THIS TRIP. SENSEI WU SAYS WE HAVE TO LEARN TO MANAGE WITHOUT POWERS FOR A WHILE, JUST IN CASE WE RUN INTO TROUBLE.
INDEED. AND I BELIEVE TROUBLE IS JUST WHAT WE HAVE FOUND.

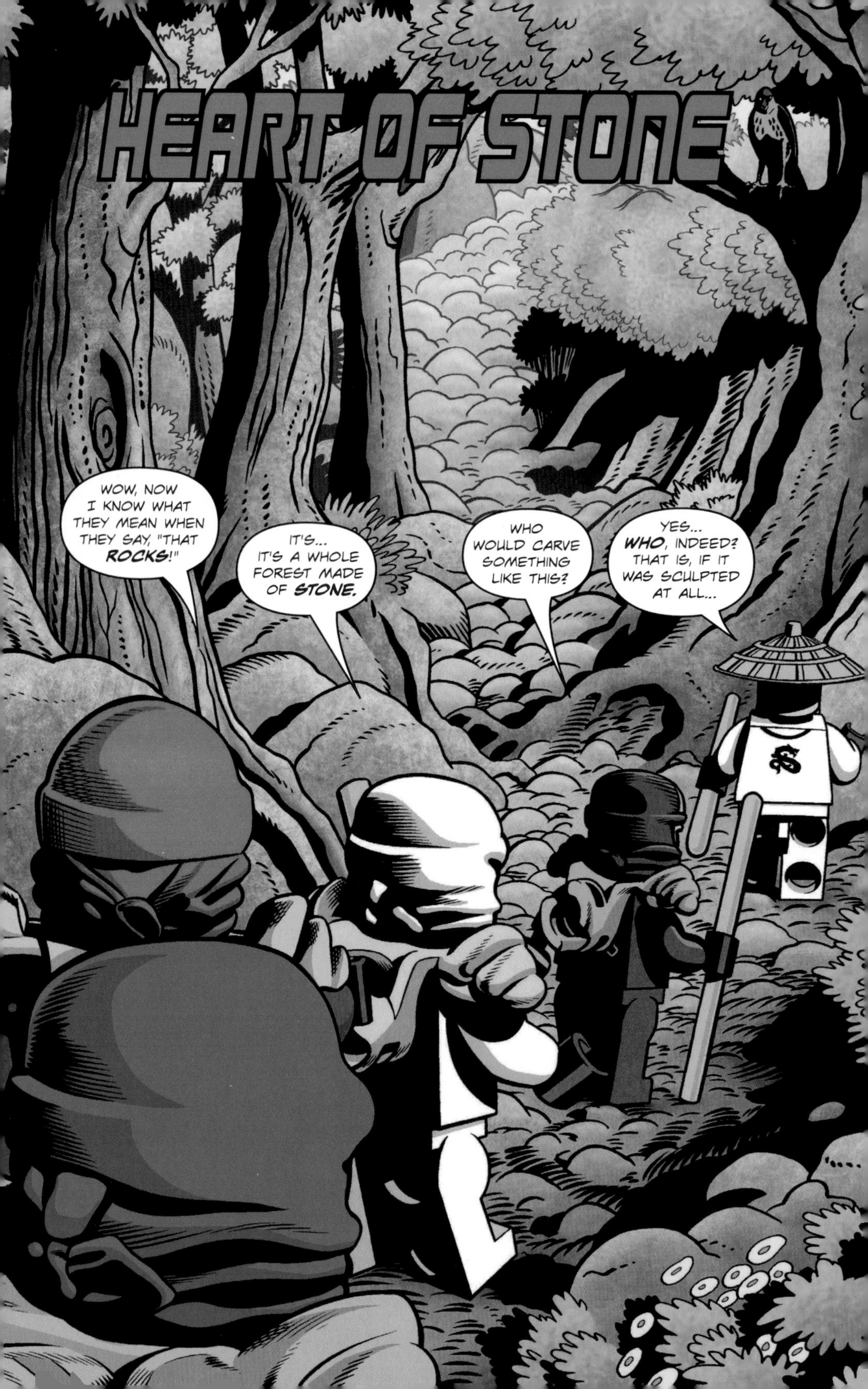
HEART OF STONE
WOW, NOW I KNOW WHAT THEY MEAN WHEN THEY SAY, "THAT ROCKS!"
IT'S... IT'S A WHOLE FOREST MADE OF STONE.
WHO WOULD CARVE SOMETHING LIKE THIS?
YES... WHO, INDEED? THAT IS, IF IT WAS SCULPTED AT ALL...

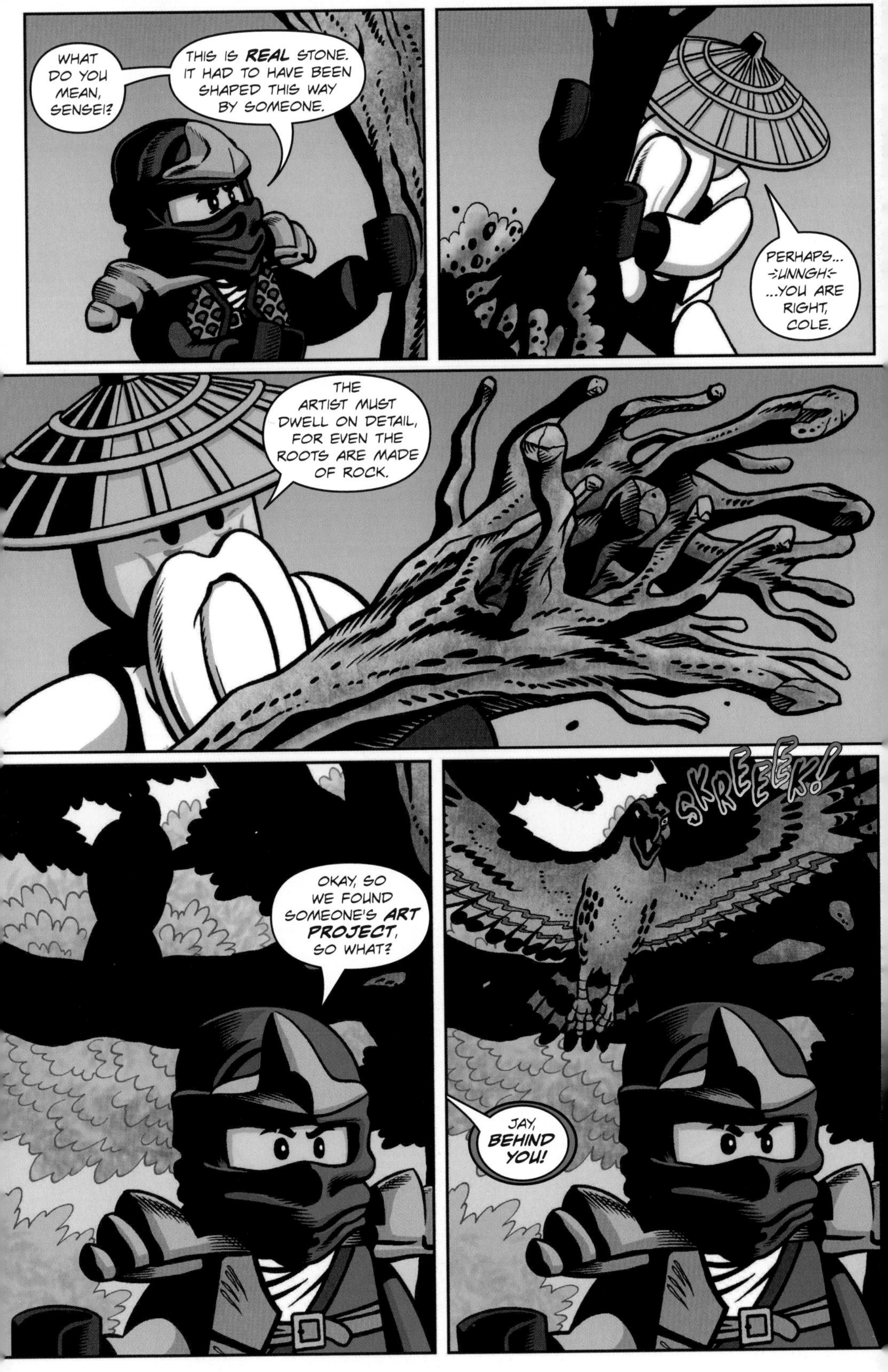
WHAT DO YOU MEAN, SENSEI?
THIS IS **REAL** STONE. IT HAD TO HAVE BEEN SHAPED THIS WAY BY SOMEONE.
PERHAPS... -UNNGH- ...YOU ARE RIGHT, COLE.
THE ARTIST MUST DWELL ON DETAIL, FOR EVEN THE ROOTS ARE MADE OF ROCK.
OKAY, SO WE FOUND SOMEONE'S **ART PROJECT**, SO WHAT?
SKREEEK!
JAY, **BEHIND YOU!**

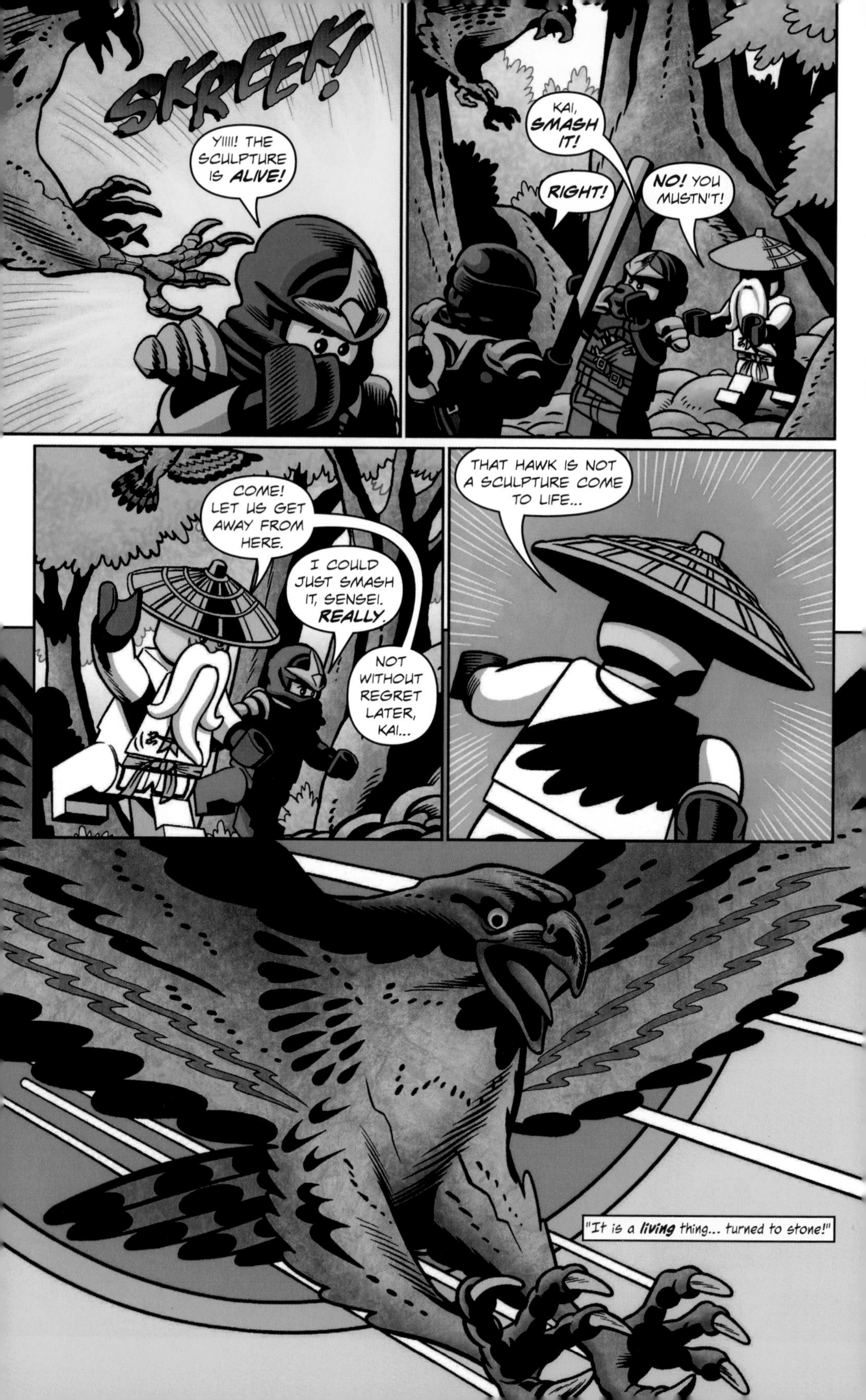

SKREEK!
YIIII! THE SCULPTURE IS ALIVE!
KAI, SMASH IT!
RIGHT!
NO! YOU MUSTN'T!
COME! LET US GET AWAY FROM HERE.
I COULD JUST SMASH IT, SENSEI. REALLY.
NOT WITHOUT REGRET LATER, KAI...
THAT HAWK IS NOT A SCULPTURE COME TO LIFE...
"It is a living thing... turned to stone!"

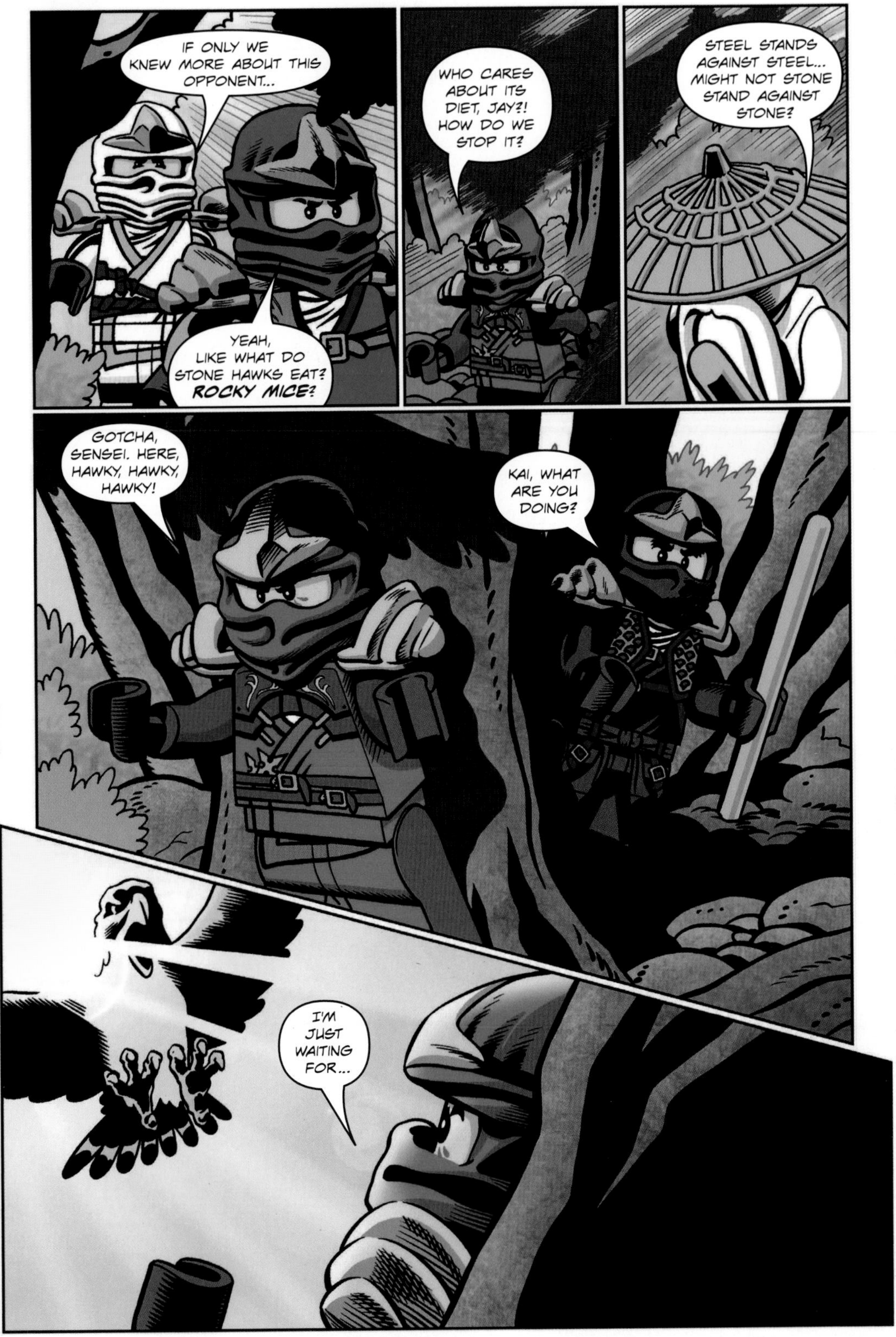
IF ONLY WE KNEW MORE ABOUT THIS OPPONENT...
YEAH, LIKE WHAT DO STONE HAWKS EAT? ROCKY MICE?
WHO CARES ABOUT ITS DIET, JAY?! HOW DO WE STOP IT?
STEEL STANDS AGAINST STEEL... MIGHT NOT STONE STAND AGAINST STONE?
GOTCHA, SENSEI. HERE, HAWKY, HAWKY, HAWKY!
KAI, WHAT ARE YOU DOING?
I'M JUST WAITING FOR...

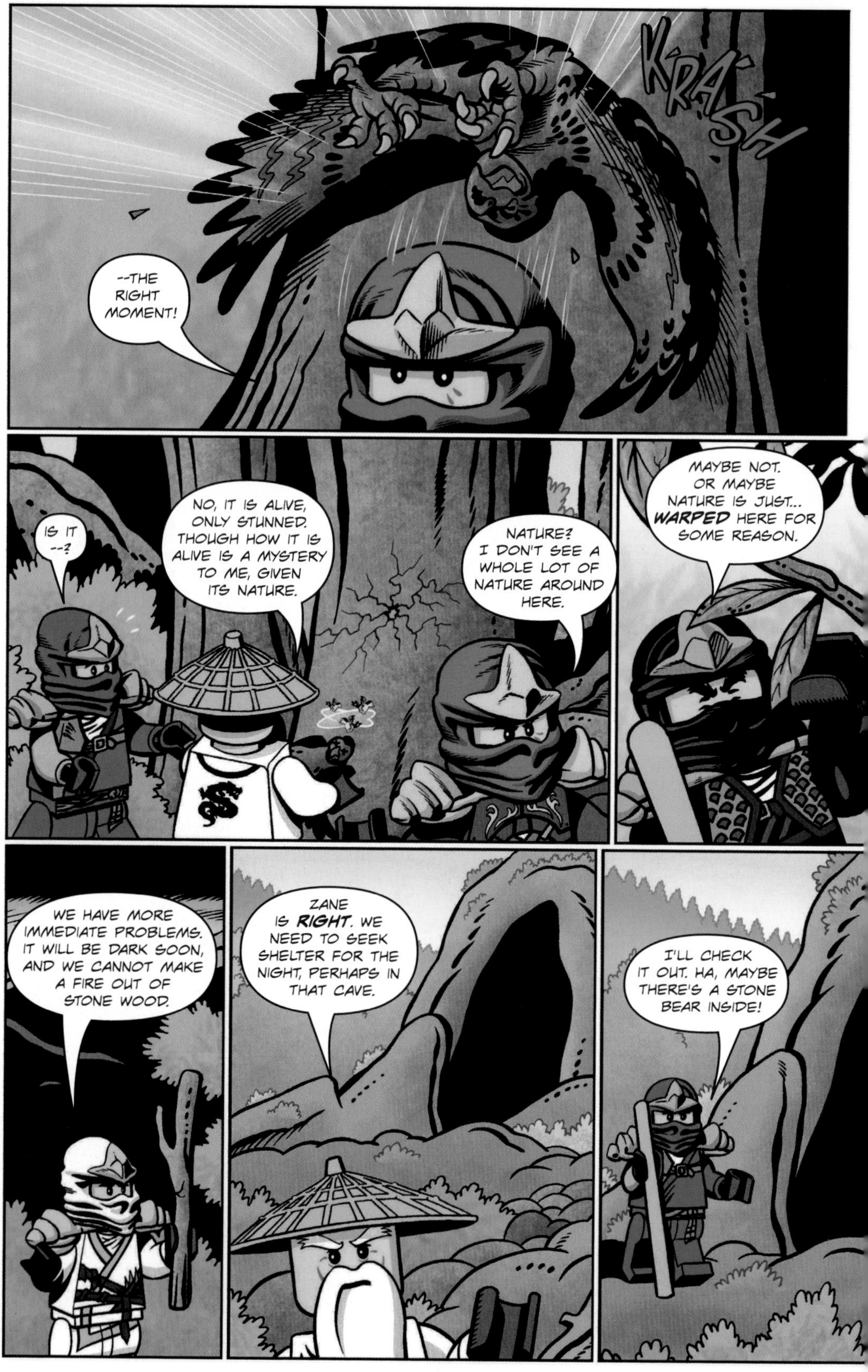
K-RA-SH
--THE RIGHT MOMENT!
IS IT --?
NO, IT IS ALIVE, ONLY STUNNED. THOUGH HOW IT IS ALIVE IS A MYSTERY TO ME, GIVEN ITS NATURE.
NATURE? I DON'T SEE A WHOLE LOT OF NATURE AROUND HERE.
MAYBE NOT. OR MAYBE NATURE IS JUST... **WARPED** HERE FOR SOME REASON.
WE HAVE MORE IMMEDIATE PROBLEMS. IT WILL BE DARK SOON, AND WE CANNOT MAKE A FIRE OUT OF STONE WOOD.
ZANE IS **RIGHT**. WE NEED TO SEEK SHELTER FOR THE NIGHT, PERHAPS IN THAT CAVE.
I'LL CHECK IT OUT. HA, MAYBE THERE'S A STONE BEAR INSIDE!

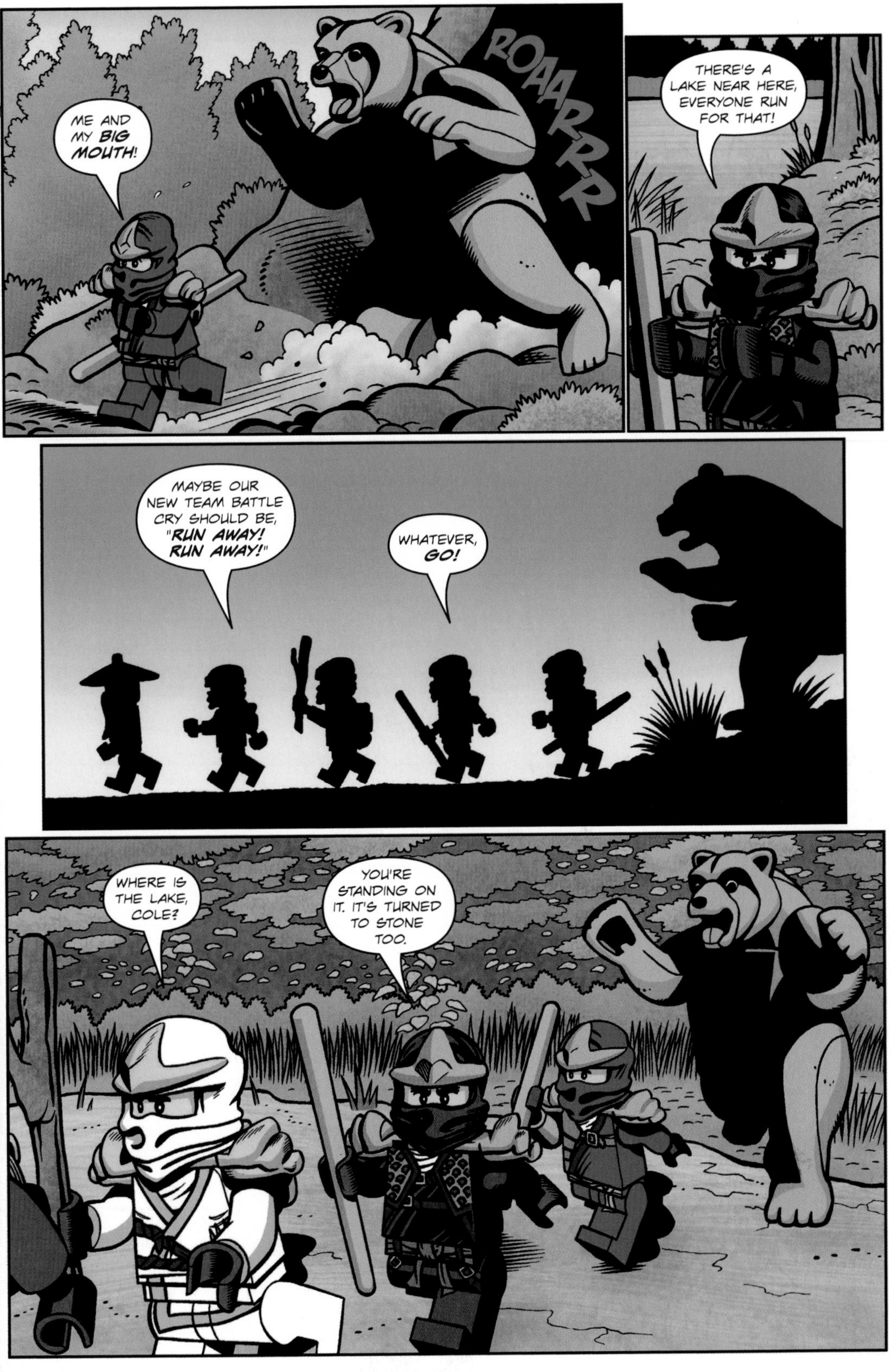
ME AND MY **BIG MOUTH**!
ROAAARRR
THERE'S A LAKE NEAR HERE, EVERYONE RUN FOR THAT!
MAYBE OUR NEW TEAM BATTLE CRY SHOULD BE, "**RUN AWAY! RUN AWAY!**"
WHATEVER, **GO!**
WHERE IS THE LAKE, COLE?
YOU'RE STANDING ON IT. IT'S TURNED TO STONE TOO.

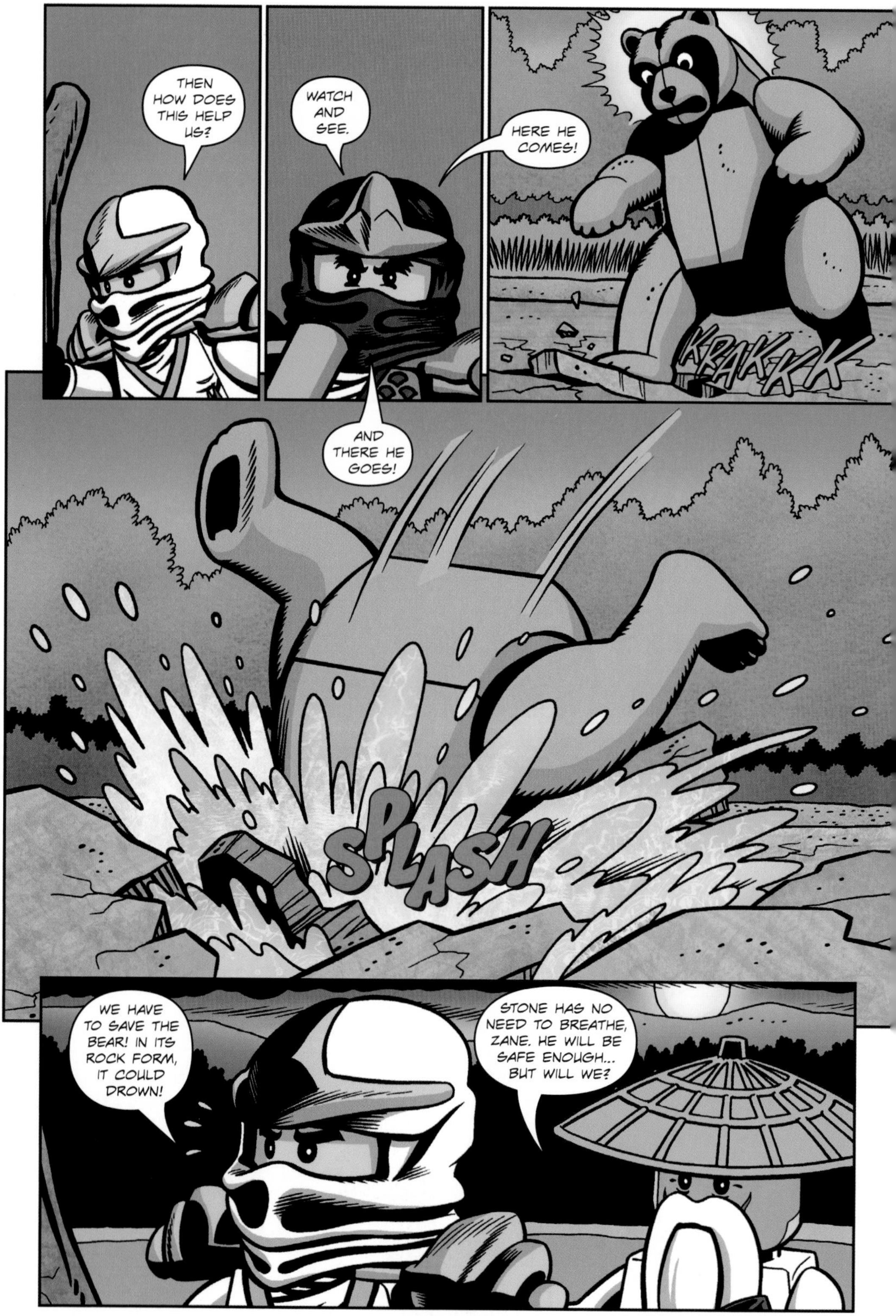
THEN HOW DOES THIS HELP US?
WATCH AND SEE.
HERE HE COMES!
KRAKKKK
AND THERE HE GOES!
SPLASH
WE HAVE TO SAVE THE BEAR! IN ITS ROCK FORM, IT COULD DROWN!
STONE HAS NO NEED TO BREATHE, ZANE. HE WILL BE SAFE ENOUGH... BUT WILL WE?

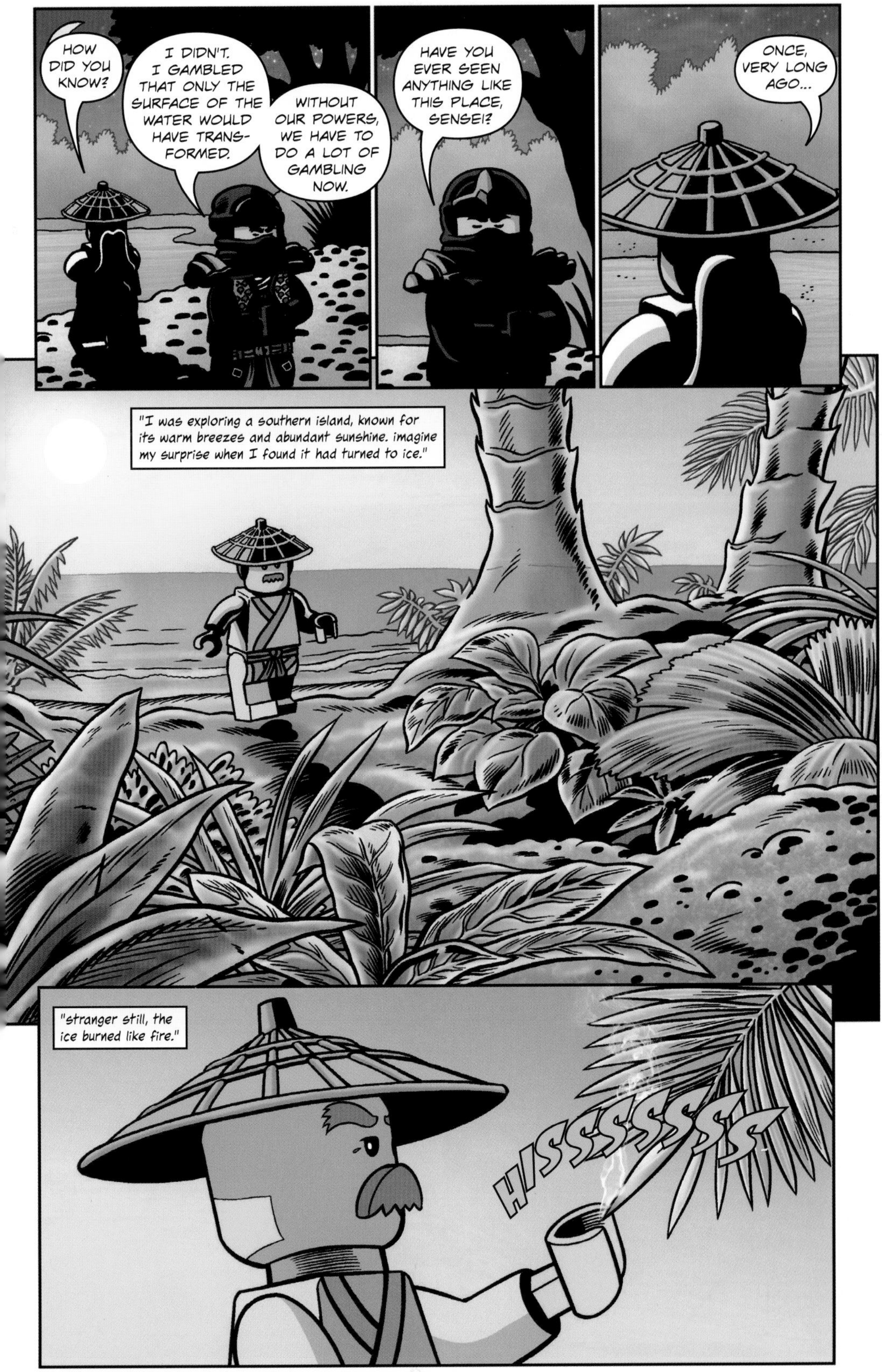
HOW DID YOU KNOW?
I DIDN'T. I GAMBLED THAT ONLY THE SURFACE OF THE WATER WOULD HAVE TRANS-FORMED.
WITHOUT OUR POWERS, WE HAVE TO DO A LOT OF GAMBLING NOW.
HAVE YOU EVER SEEN ANYTHING LIKE THIS PLACE, SENSEI?
ONCE, VERY LONG AGO...
"I was exploring a southern island, known for its warm breezes and abundant sunshine. imagine my surprise when I found it had turned to ice."
"stranger still, the ice burned like fire."
HISSSSSSS

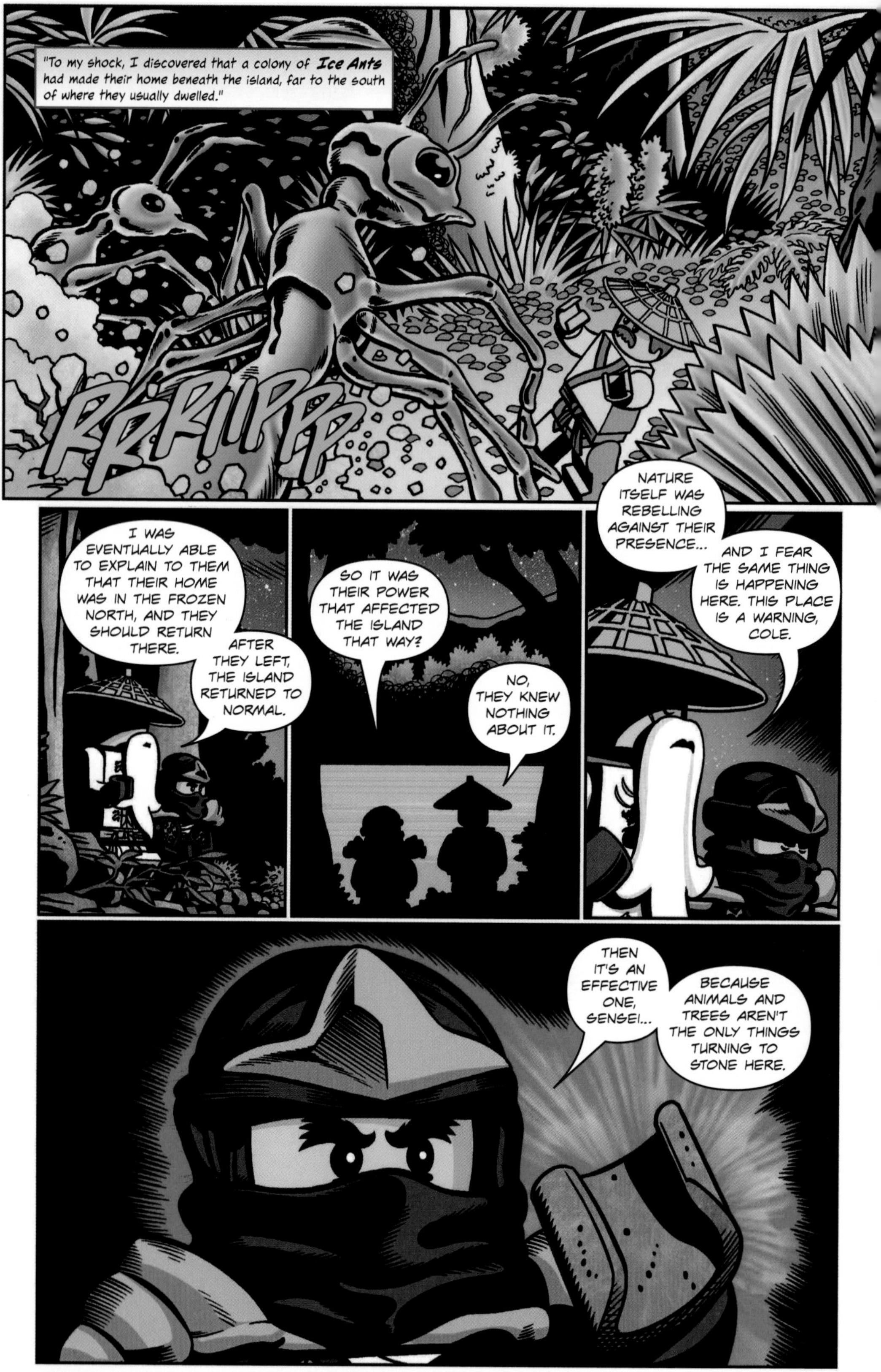
"To my shock, I discovered that a colony of Ice Ants had made their home beneath the island, far to the south of where they usually dwelled."
RRRIIPPP
I WAS EVENTUALLY ABLE TO EXPLAIN TO THEM THAT THEIR HOME WAS IN THE FROZEN NORTH, AND THEY SHOULD RETURN THERE.
AFTER THEY LEFT, THE ISLAND RETURNED TO NORMAL.
SO IT WAS THEIR POWER THAT AFFECTED THE ISLAND THAT WAY?
NO, THEY KNEW NOTHING ABOUT IT.
NATURE ITSELF WAS REBELLING AGAINST THEIR PRESENCE...
AND I FEAR THE SAME THING IS HAPPENING HERE. THIS PLACE IS A WARNING, COLE.
THEN IT'S AN EFFECTIVE ONE, SENSEI...
BECAUSE ANIMALS AND TREES AREN'T THE ONLY THINGS TURNING TO STONE HERE.

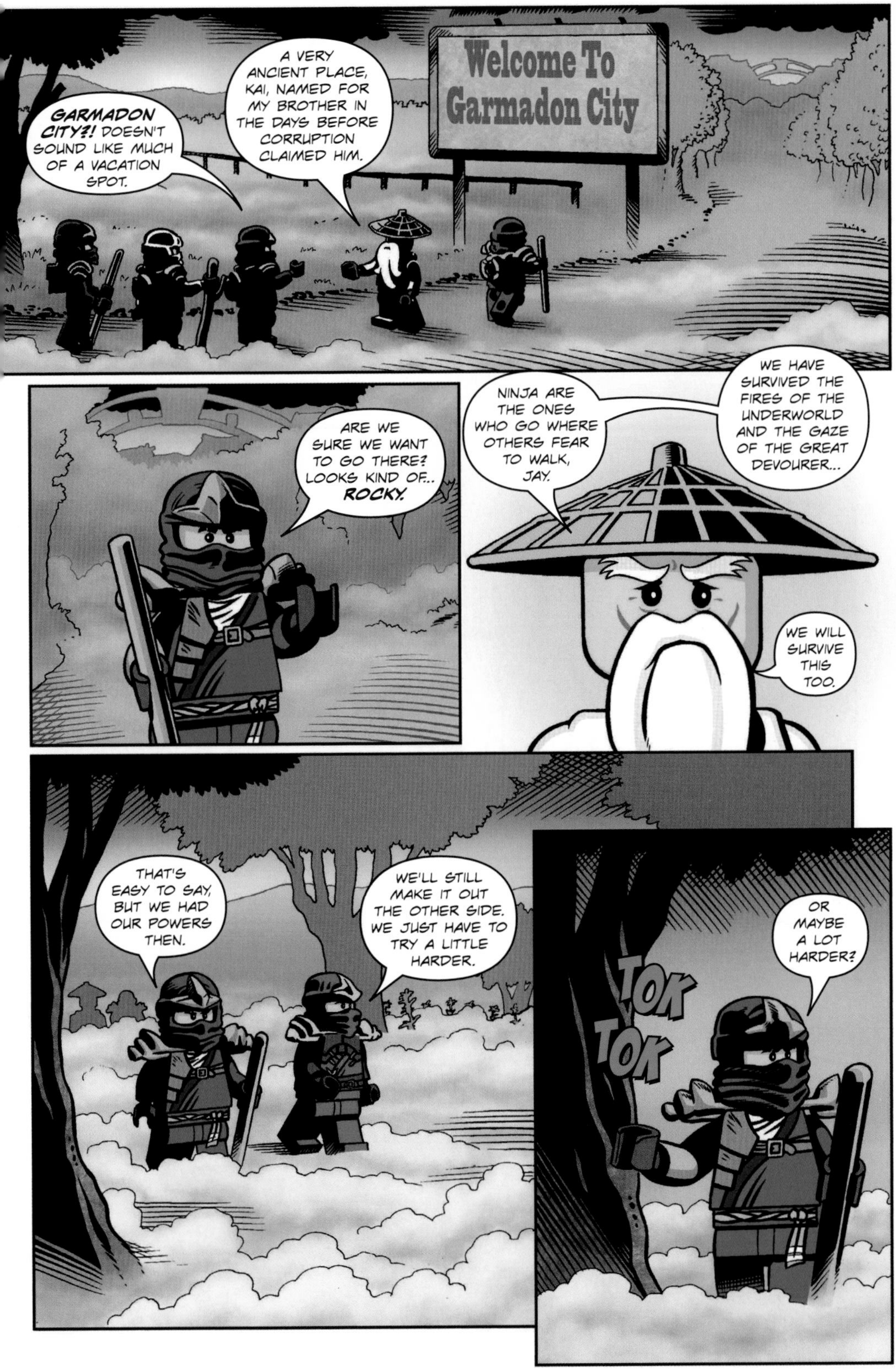
Welcome To Garmadon City
GARMADON CITY?! DOESN'T SOUND LIKE MUCH OF A VACATION SPOT.
A VERY ANCIENT PLACE, KAI, NAMED FOR MY BROTHER IN THE DAYS BEFORE CORRUPTION CLAIMED HIM.
ARE WE SURE WE WANT TO GO THERE? LOOKS KIND OF... ROCKY.
NINJA ARE THE ONES WHO GO WHERE OTHERS FEAR TO WALK, JAY.
WE HAVE SURVIVED THE FIRES OF THE UNDERWORLD AND THE GAZE OF THE GREAT DEVOURER...
WE WILL SURVIVE THIS TOO.
THAT'S EASY TO SAY, BUT WE HAD OUR POWERS THEN.
WE'LL STILL MAKE IT OUT THE OTHER SIDE. WE JUST HAVE TO TRY A LITTLE HARDER.
TOK TOK
OR MAYBE A LOT HARDER?

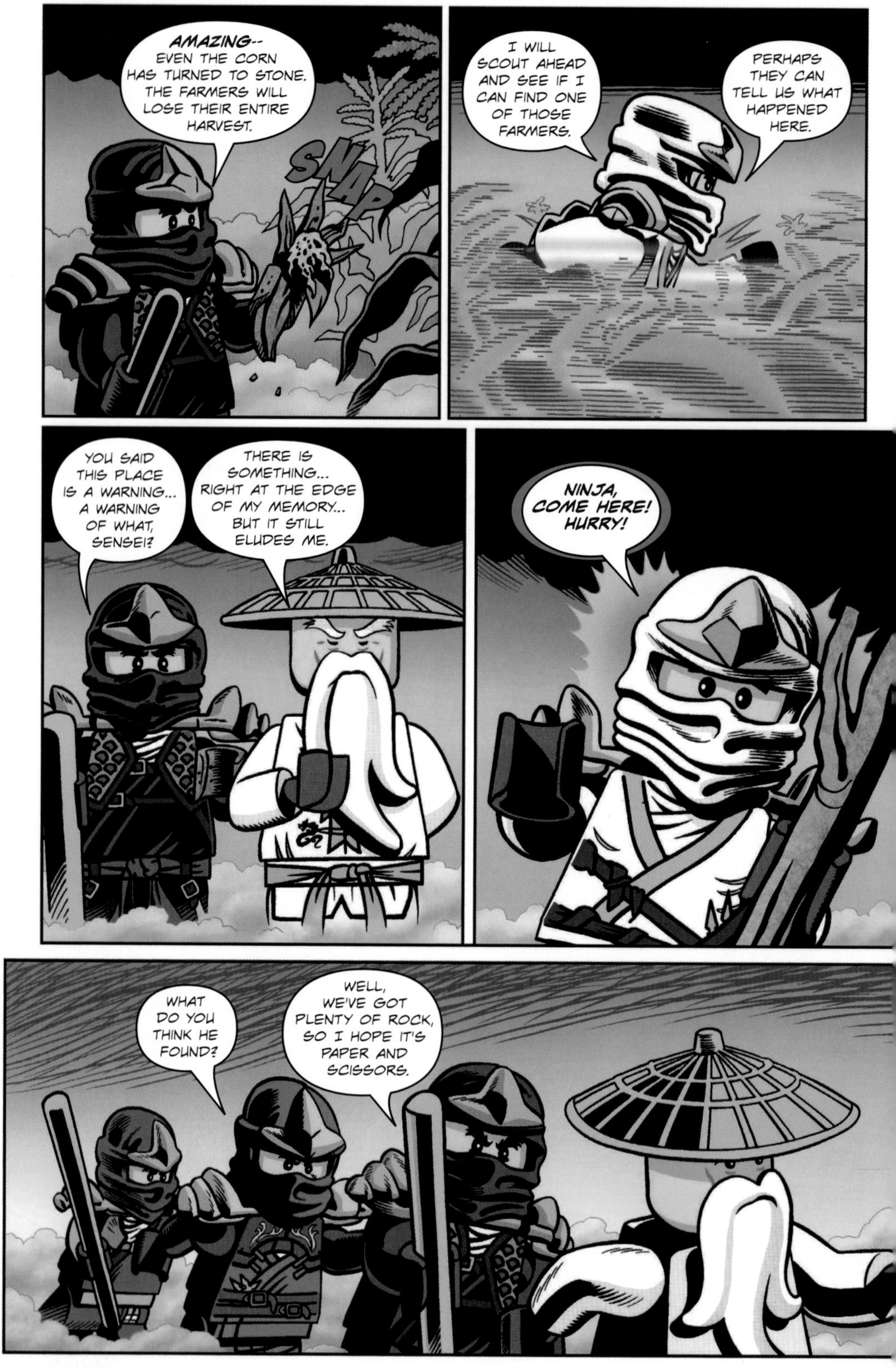
AMAZING-- EVEN THE CORN HAS TURNED TO STONE. THE FARMERS WILL LOSE THEIR ENTIRE HARVEST.
SNAP
I WILL SCOUT AHEAD AND SEE IF I CAN FIND ONE OF THOSE FARMERS.
PERHAPS THEY CAN TELL US WHAT HAPPENED HERE.
YOU SAID THIS PLACE IS A WARNING... A WARNING OF WHAT, SENSEI?
THERE IS SOMETHING... RIGHT AT THE EDGE OF MY MEMORY... BUT IT STILL ELUDES ME.
NINJA, COME HERE! HURRY!
WHAT DO YOU THINK HE FOUND?
WELL, WE'VE GOT PLENTY OF ROCK, SO I HOPE IT'S PAPER AND SCISSORS.

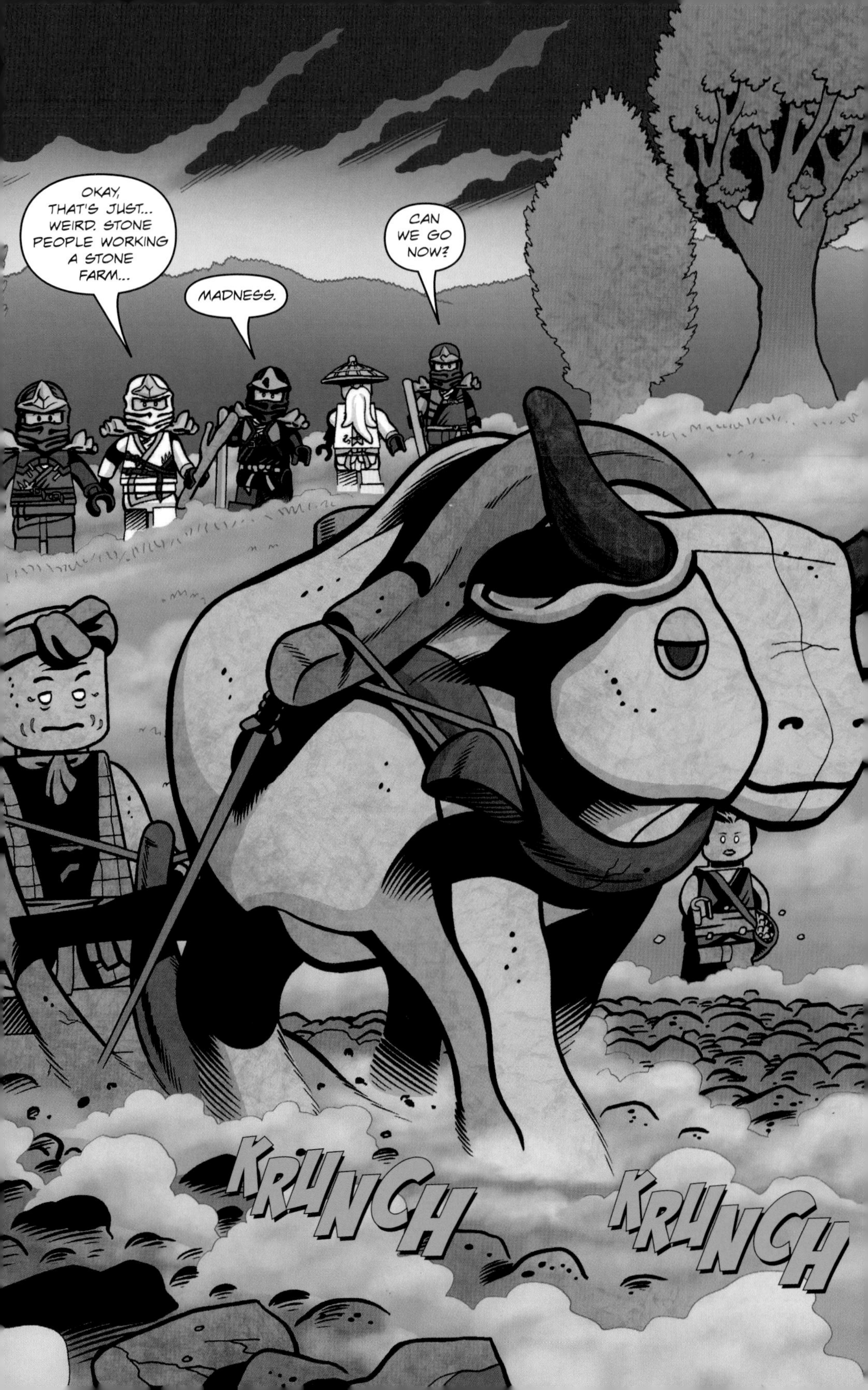
OKAY, THAT'S JUST... WEIRD. STONE PEOPLE WORKING A STONE FARM...
MADNESS.
CAN WE GO NOW?
KRUNCH
KRUNCH

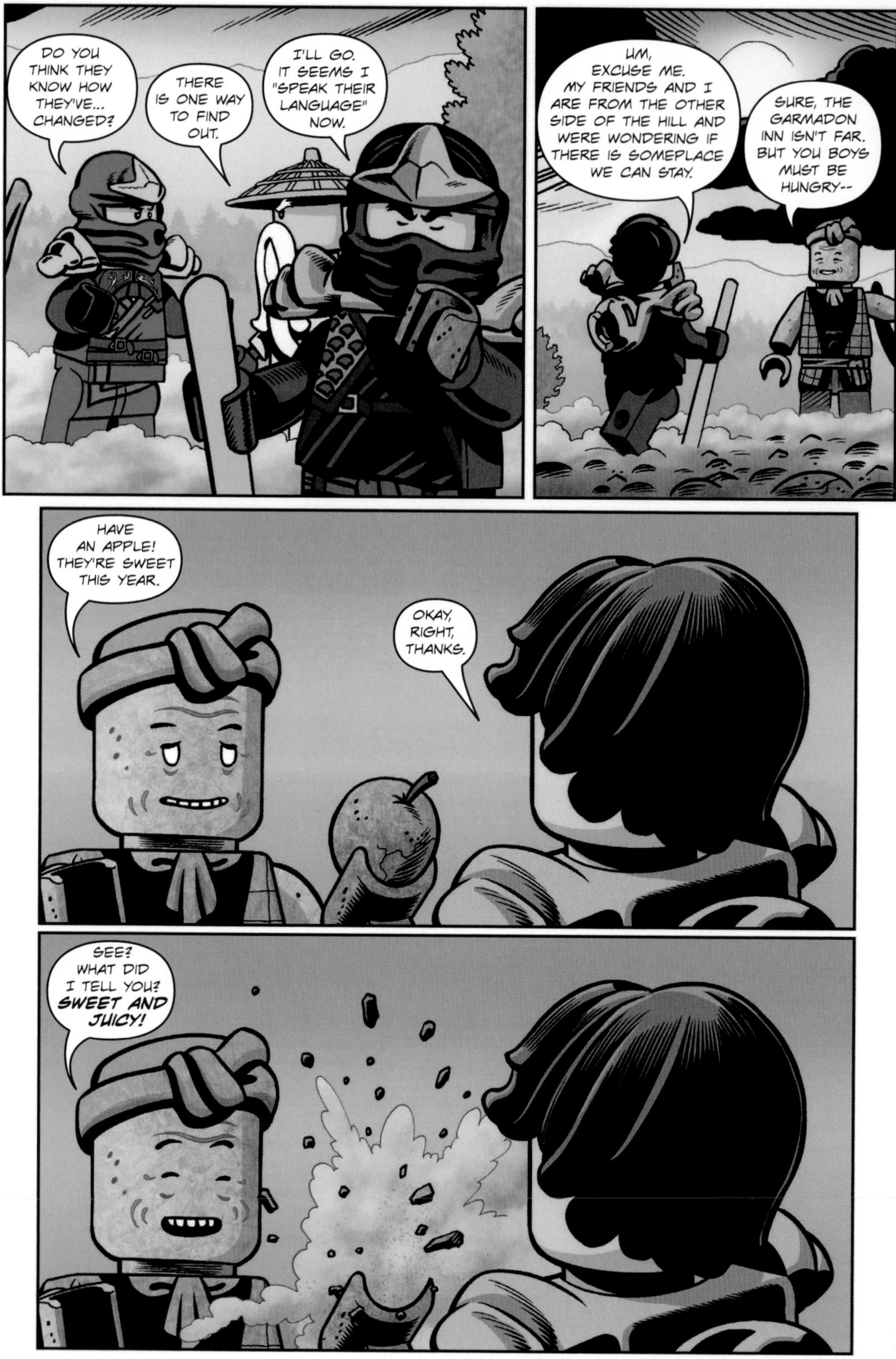
DO YOU THINK THEY KNOW HOW THEY'VE... CHANGED?
THERE IS ONE WAY TO FIND OUT.
I'LL GO. IT SEEMS I "SPEAK THEIR LANGUAGE" NOW.
UM, EXCUSE ME. MY FRIENDS AND I ARE FROM THE OTHER SIDE OF THE HILL AND WERE WONDERING IF THERE IS SOMEPLACE WE CAN STAY.
SURE, THE GARMADON INN ISN'T FAR. BUT YOU BOYS MUST BE HUNGRY--
HAVE AN APPLE! THEY'RE SWEET THIS YEAR.
OKAY, RIGHT, THANKS.
SEE? WHAT DID I TELL YOU? SWEET AND JUICY!

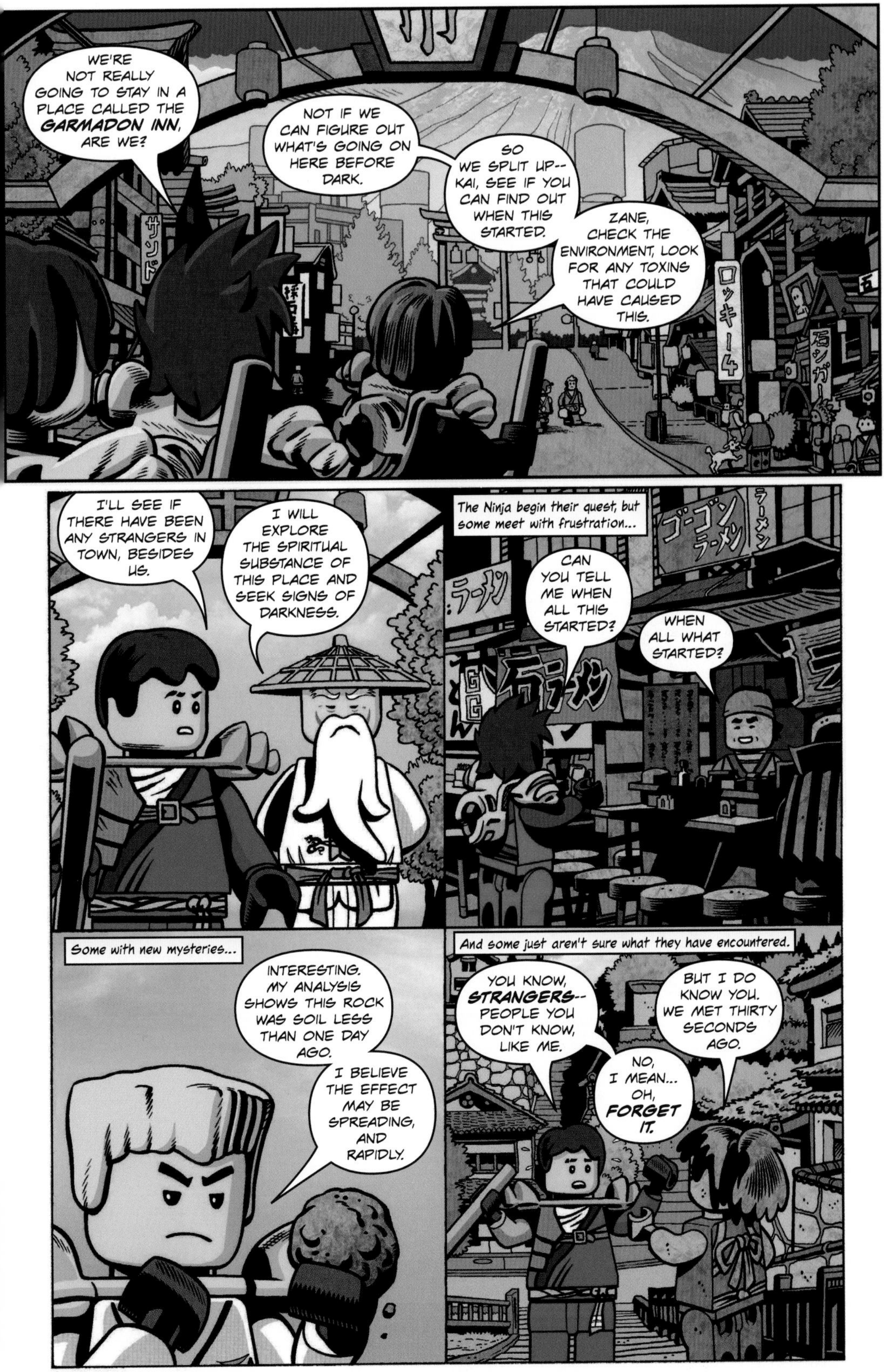
WE'RE NOT REALLY GOING TO STAY IN A PLACE CALLED THE GARMADON INN, ARE WE?
NOT IF WE CAN FIGURE OUT WHAT'S GOING ON HERE BEFORE DARK.
SO WE SPLIT UP-- KAI, SEE IF YOU CAN FIND OUT WHEN THIS STARTED.
ZANE, CHECK THE ENVIRONMENT, LOOK FOR ANY TOXINS THAT COULD HAVE CAUSED THIS.
I'LL SEE IF THERE HAVE BEEN ANY STRANGERS IN TOWN, BESIDES US.
I WILL EXPLORE THE SPIRITUAL SUBSTANCE OF THIS PLACE AND SEEK SIGNS OF DARKNESS.
The Ninja begin their quest, but some meet with frustration...
CAN YOU TELL ME WHEN ALL THIS STARTED?
WHEN ALL WHAT STARTED?
Some with new mysteries...
INTERESTING. MY ANALYSIS SHOWS THIS ROCK WAS SOIL LESS THAN ONE DAY AGO.
I BELIEVE THE EFFECT MAY BE SPREADING, AND RAPIDLY.
And some just aren't sure what they have encountered.
YOU KNOW, STRANGERS-- PEOPLE YOU DON'T KNOW, LIKE ME.
BUT I DO KNOW YOU. WE MET THIRTY SECONDS AGO.
NO, I MEAN... OH, FORGET IT.

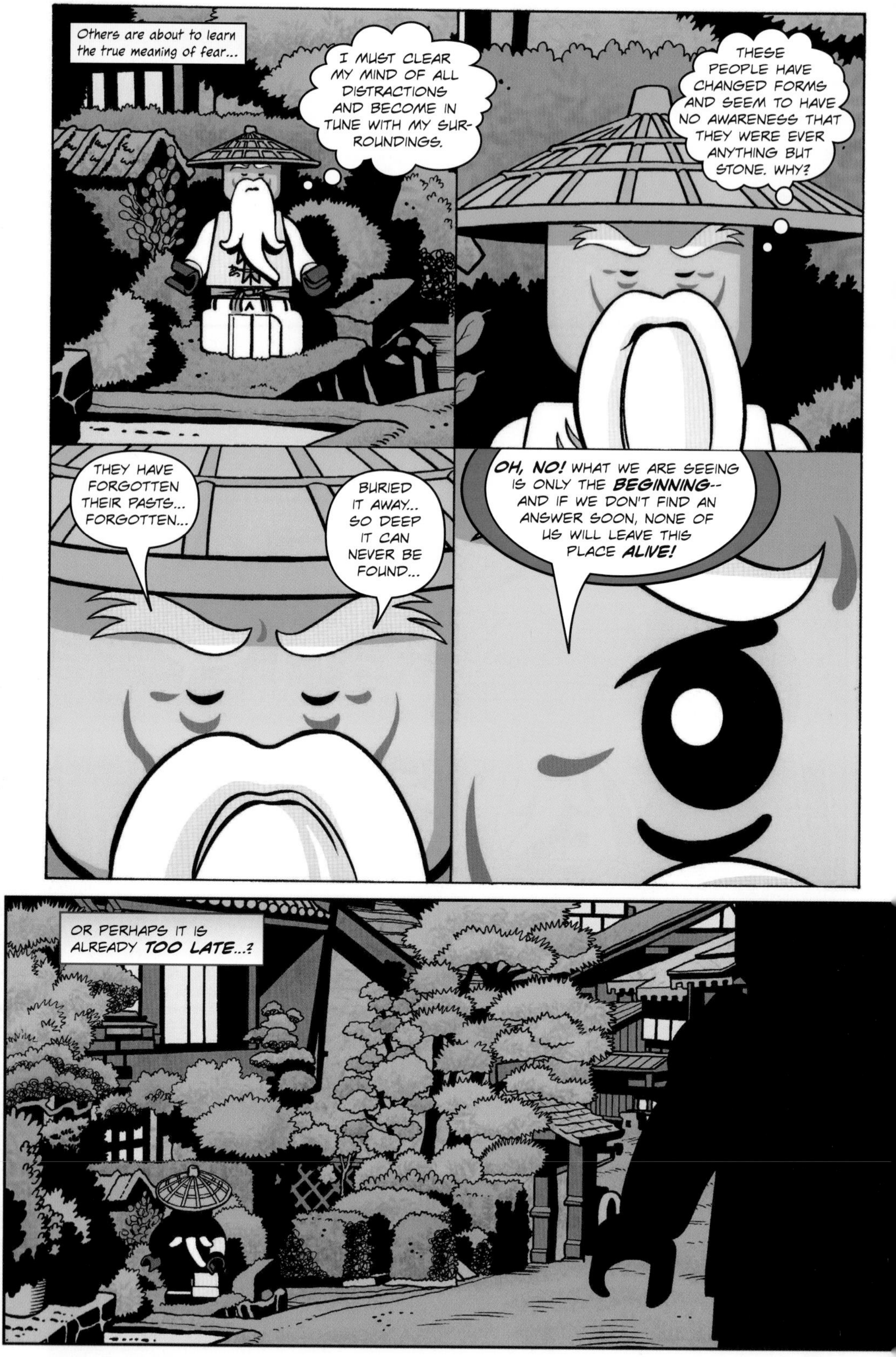
Others are about to learn the true meaning of fear...
I MUST CLEAR MY MIND OF ALL DISTRACTIONS AND BECOME IN TUNE WITH MY SURROUNDINGS.
THESE PEOPLE HAVE CHANGED FORMS AND SEEM TO HAVE NO AWARENESS THAT THEY WERE EVER ANYTHING BUT STONE. WHY?
THEY HAVE FORGOTTEN THEIR PASTS... FORGOTTEN...
BURIED IT AWAY... SO DEEP IT CAN NEVER BE FOUND...
OH, NO! WHAT WE ARE SEEING IS ONLY THE BEGINNING-- AND IF WE DON'T FIND AN ANSWER SOON, NONE OF US WILL LEAVE THIS PLACE ALIVE!
OR PERHAPS IT IS ALREADY TOO LATE...?

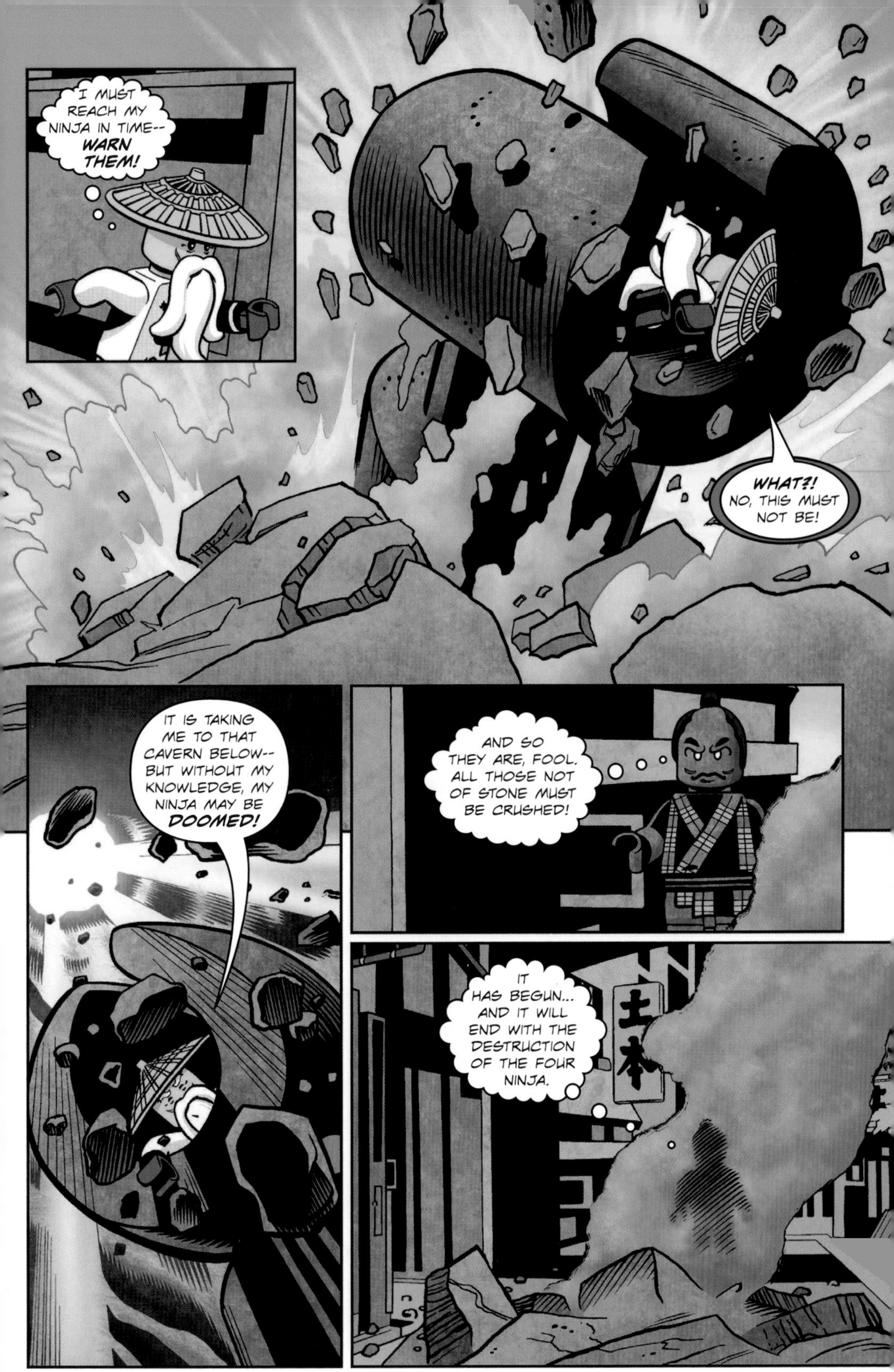
I MUST REACH MY NINJA IN TIME-- WARN THEM!
WHAT?! NO, THIS MUST NOT BE!
IT IS TAKING ME TO THAT CAVERN BELOW-- BUT WITHOUT MY KNOWLEDGE, MY NINJA MAY BE DOOMED!
AND SO THEY ARE, FOOL. ALL THOSE NOT OF STONE MUST BE CRUSHED!
IT HAS BEGUN... AND IT WILL END WITH THE DESTRUCTION OF THE FOUR NINJA.

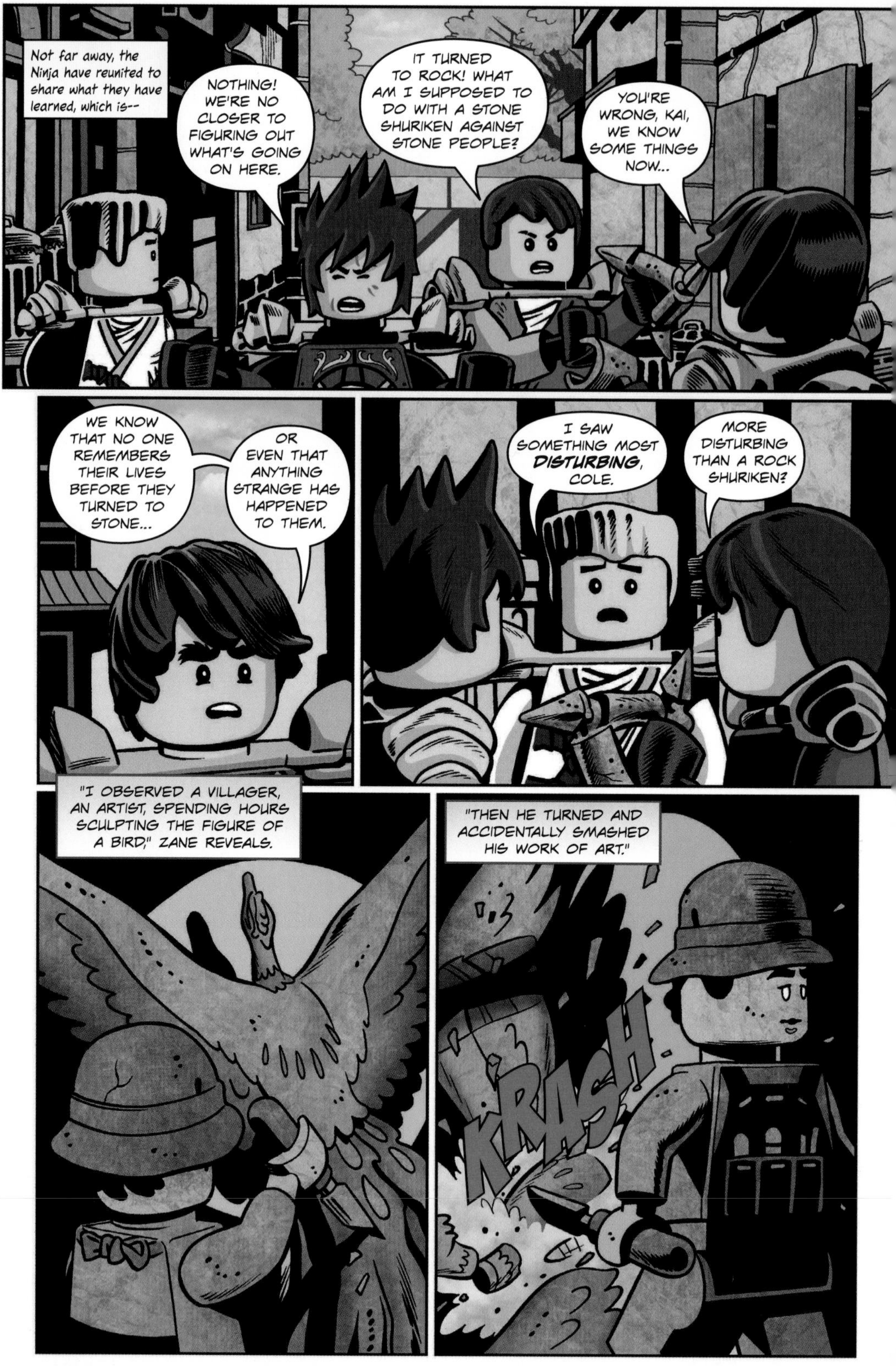

Not far away, the Ninja have reunited to share what they have learned, which is--
NOTHING! WE'RE NO CLOSER TO FIGURING OUT WHAT'S GOING ON HERE.
IT TURNED TO ROCK! WHAT AM I SUPPOSED TO DO WITH A STONE SHURIKEN AGAINST STONE PEOPLE?
YOU'RE WRONG, KAI, WE KNOW SOME THINGS NOW...
WE KNOW THAT NO ONE REMEMBERS THEIR LIVES BEFORE THEY TURNED TO STONE...
OR EVEN THAT ANYTHING STRANGE HAS HAPPENED TO THEM.
I SAW SOMETHING MOST DISTURBING, COLE.
MORE DISTURBING THAN A ROCK SHURIKEN?
"I OBSERVED A VILLAGER, AN ARTIST, SPENDING HOURS SCULPTING THE FIGURE OF A BIRD," ZANE REVEALS.
"THEN HE TURNED AND ACCIDENTALLY SMASHED HIS WORK OF ART."
KRASH

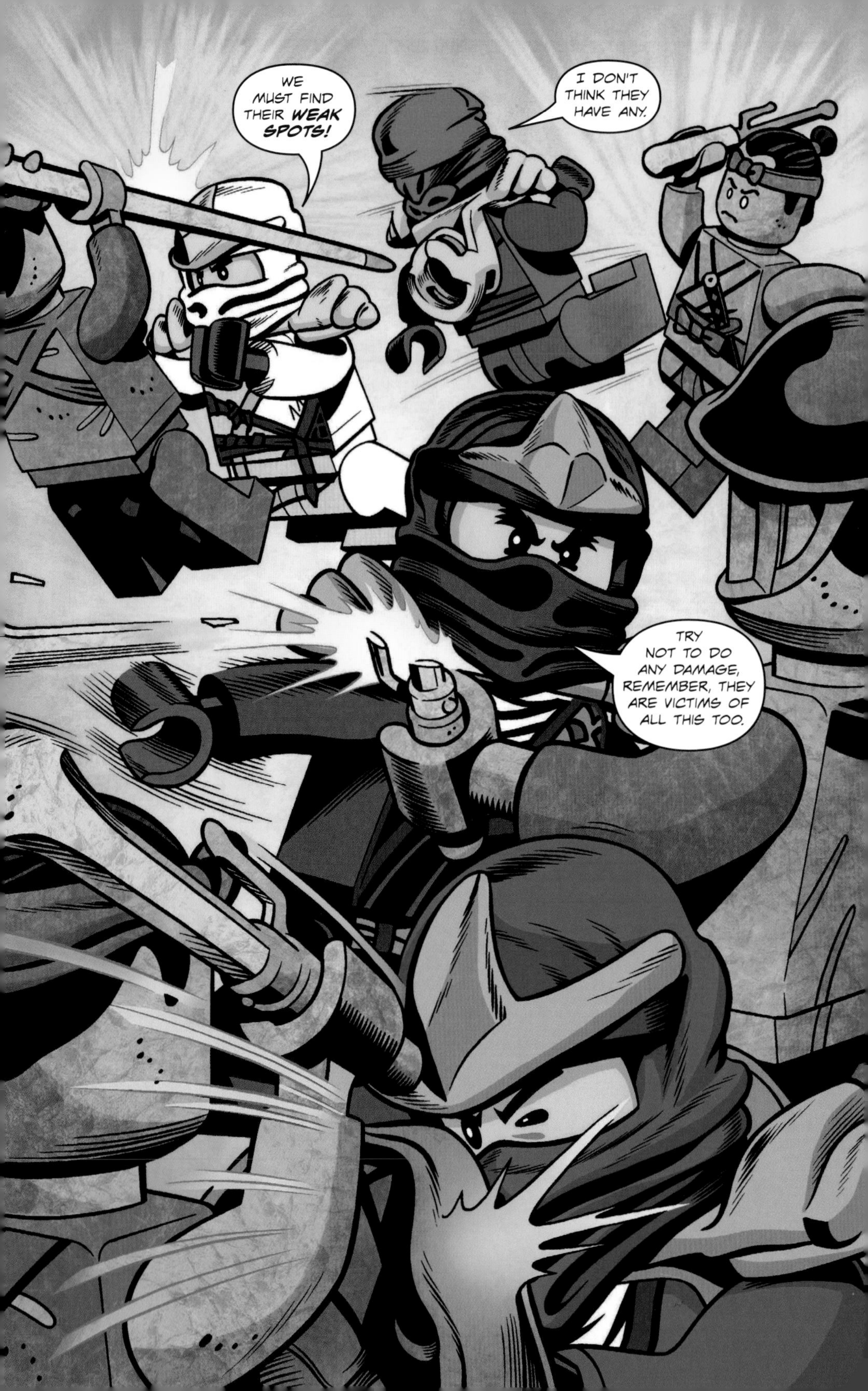
WE MUST FIND THEIR WEAK SPOTS!
I DON'T THINK THEY HAVE ANY.
TRY NOT TO DO ANY DAMAGE, REMEMBER, THEY ARE VICTIMS OF ALL THIS TOO.

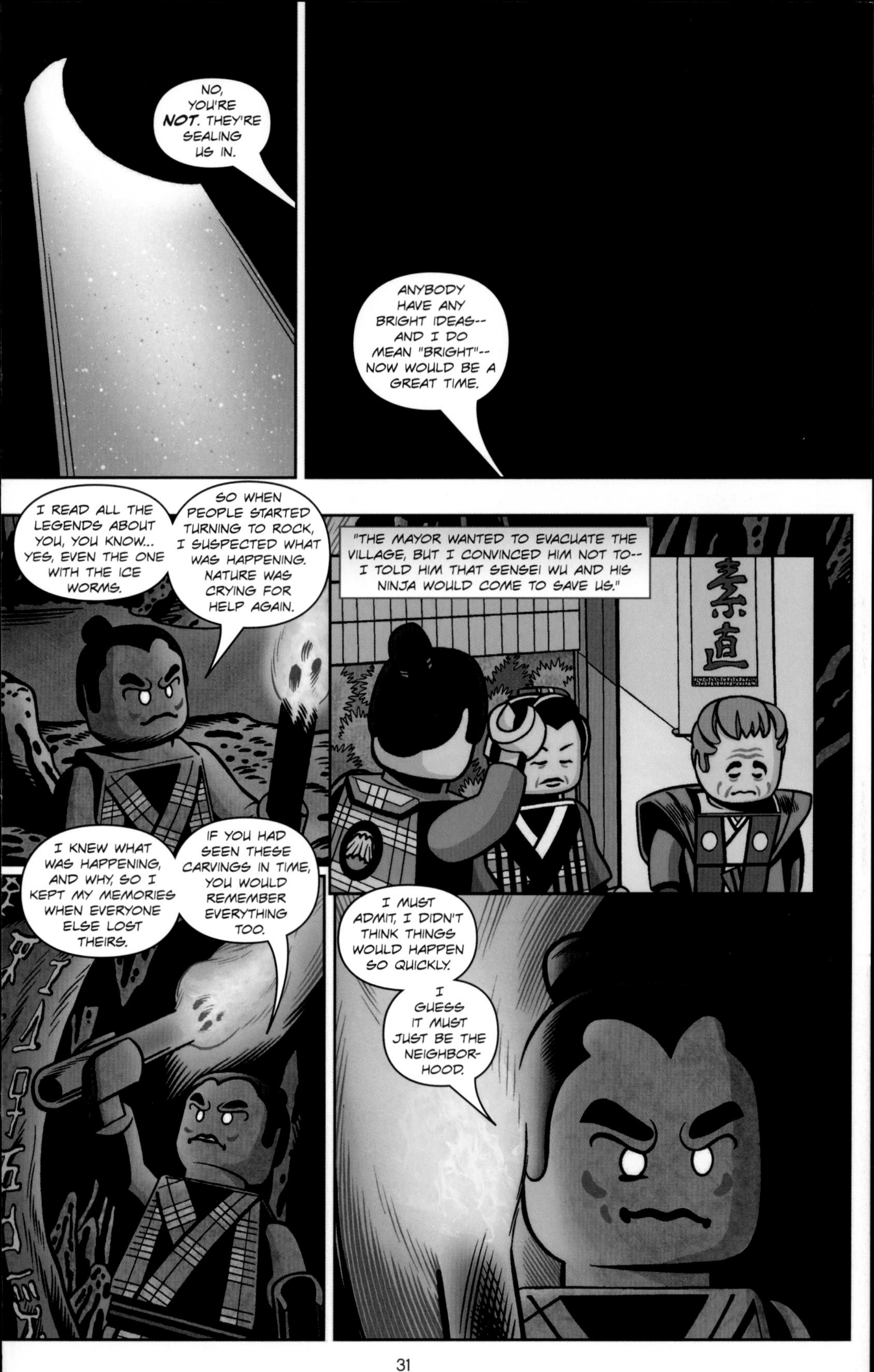
NO, YOU'RE NOT. THEY'RE SEALING US IN.
ANYBODY HAVE ANY BRIGHT IDEAS-- AND I DO MEAN "BRIGHT"-- NOW WOULD BE A GREAT TIME.
I READ ALL THE LEGENDS ABOUT YOU, YOU KNOW... YES, EVEN THE ONE WITH THE ICE WORMS.
SO WHEN PEOPLE STARTED TURNING TO ROCK, I SUSPECTED WHAT WAS HAPPENING. NATURE WAS CRYING FOR HELP AGAIN.
"THE MAYOR WANTED TO EVACUATE THE VILLAGE, BUT I CONVINCED HIM NOT TO-- I TOLD HIM THAT SENSEI WU AND HIS NINJA WOULD COME TO SAVE US."
I KNEW WHAT WAS HAPPENING, AND WHY, SO I KEPT MY MEMORIES WHEN EVERYONE ELSE LOST THEIRS.
IF YOU HAD SEEN THESE CARVINGS IN TIME, YOU WOULD REMEMBER EVERYTHING TOO.
I MUST ADMIT, I DIDN'T THINK THINGS WOULD HAPPEN SO QUICKLY.
I GUESS IT MUST JUST BE THE NEIGHBOR-HOOD.

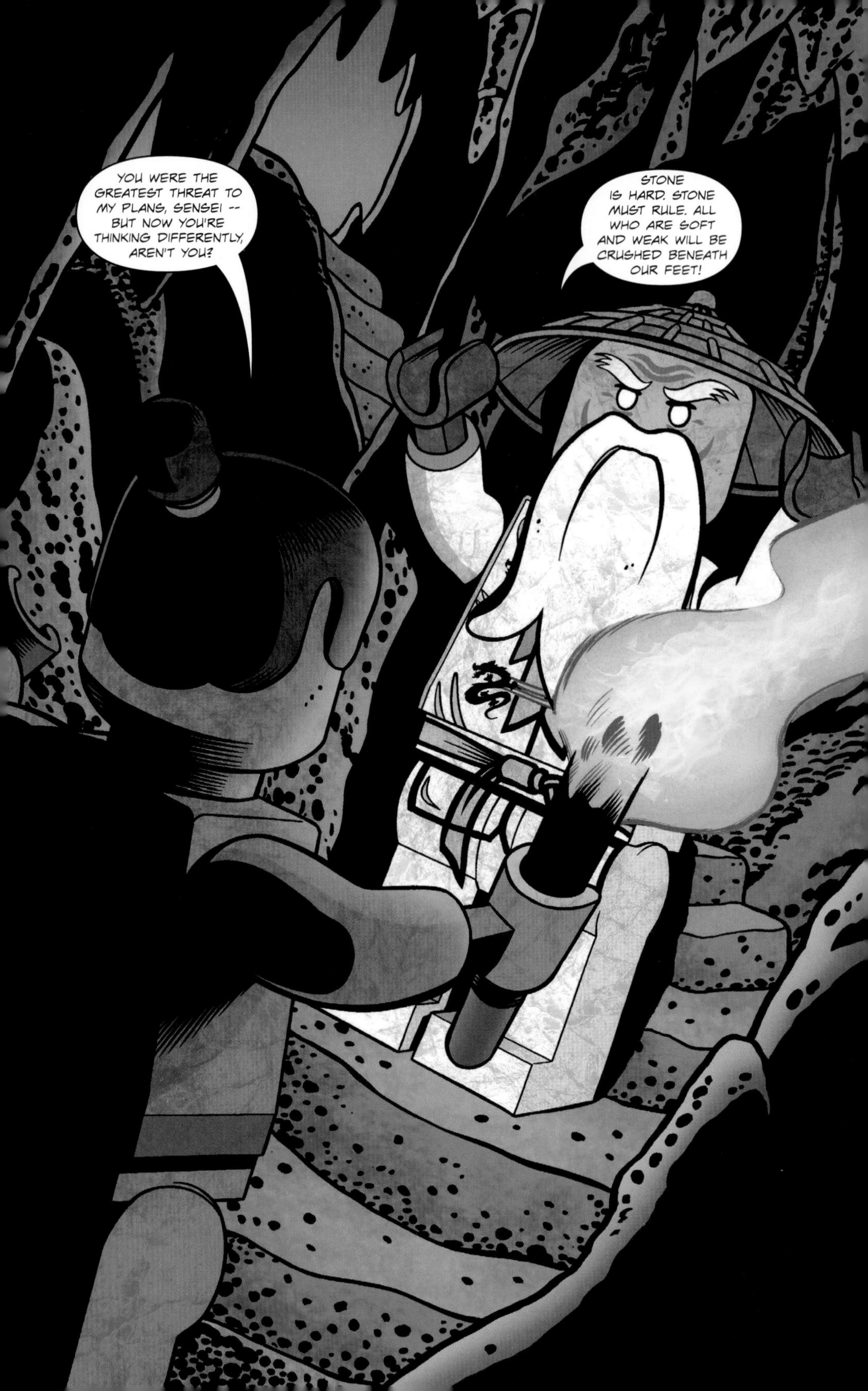
YOU WERE THE GREATEST THREAT TO MY PLANS, SENSEI -- BUT NOW YOU'RE THINKING DIFFERENTLY, AREN'T YOU?
STONE IS HARD. STONE MUST RULE. ALL WHO ARE SOFT AND WEAK WILL BE CRUSHED BENEATH OUR FEET!

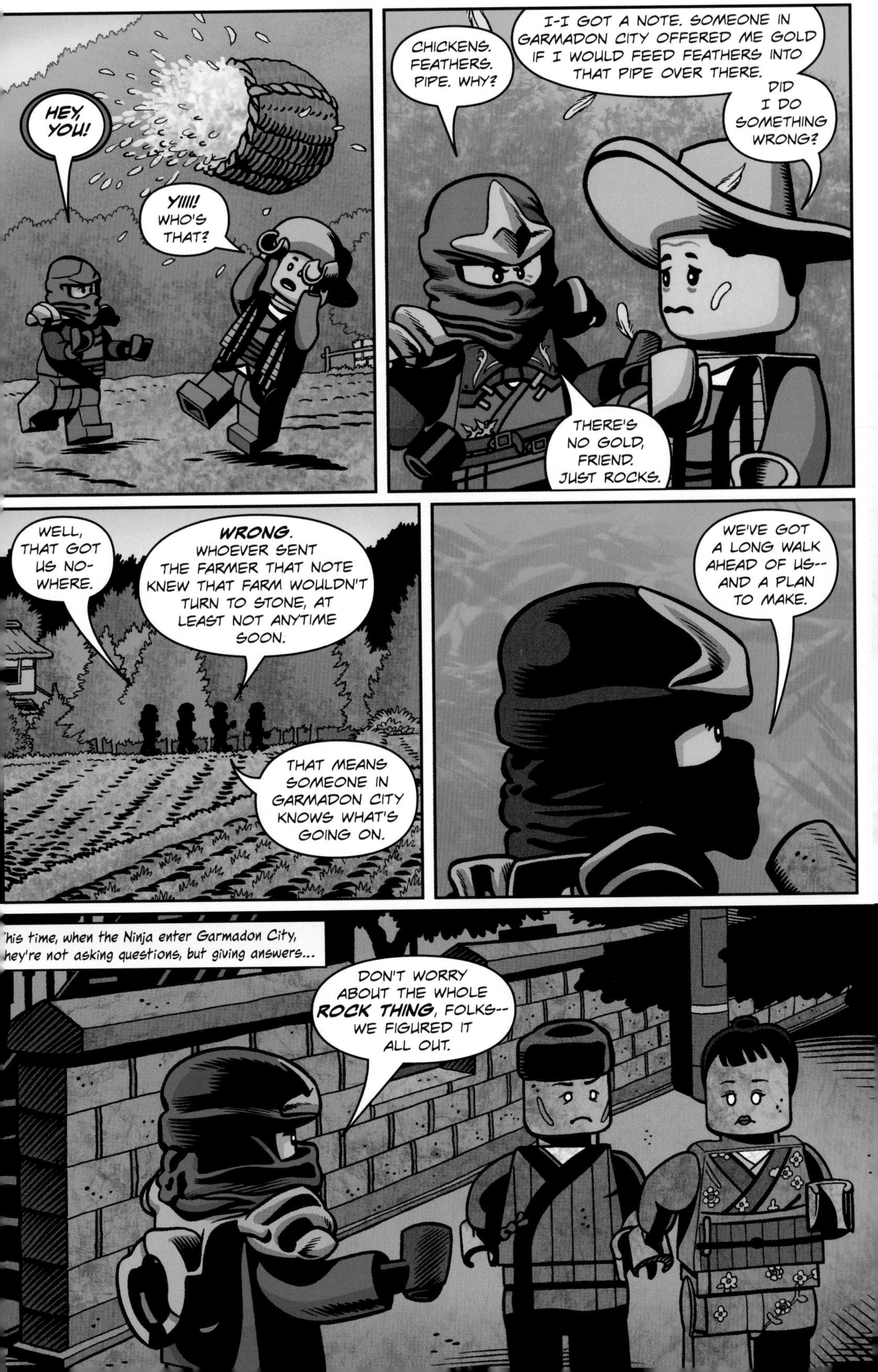
HEY, YOU!
YIIII! WHO'S THAT?
CHICKENS. FEATHERS. PIPE. WHY?
I-I GOT A NOTE. SOMEONE IN GARMADON CITY OFFERED ME GOLD IF I WOULD FEED FEATHERS INTO THAT PIPE OVER THERE.
DID I DO SOMETHING WRONG?
THERE'S NO GOLD, FRIEND. JUST ROCKS.
WELL, THAT GOT US NO-WHERE.
WRONG. WHOEVER SENT THE FARMER THAT NOTE KNEW THAT FARM WOULDN'T TURN TO STONE, AT LEAST NOT ANYTIME SOON.
THAT MEANS SOMEONE IN GARMADON CITY KNOWS WHAT'S GOING ON.
WE'VE GOT A LONG WALK AHEAD OF US-- AND A PLAN TO MAKE.
his time, when the Ninja enter Garmadon City, hey're not asking questions, but giving answers...
DON'T WORRY ABOUT THE WHOLE ROCK THING, FOLKS-- WE FIGURED IT ALL OUT.

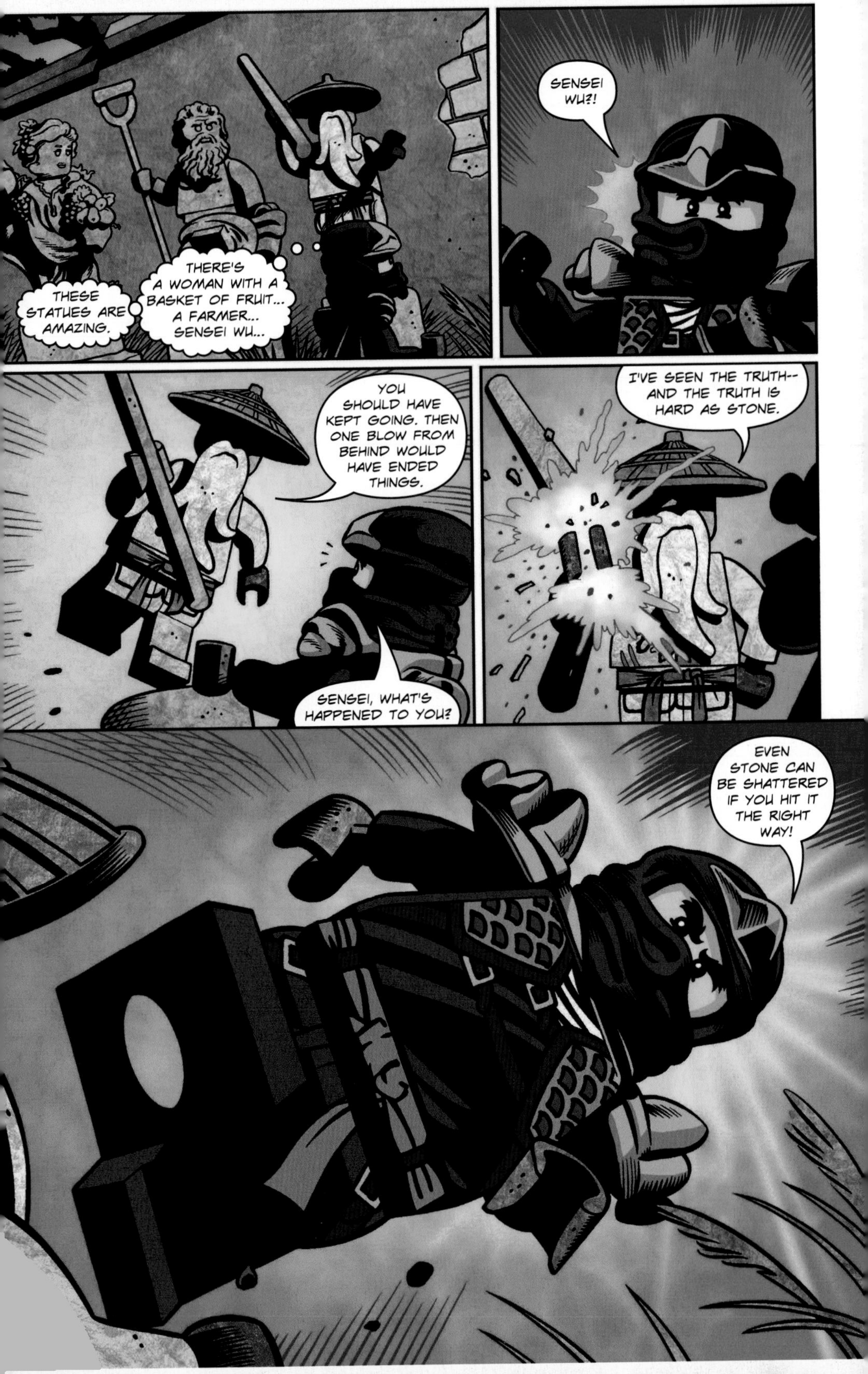
THESE STATUES ARE AMAZING.
THERE'S A WOMAN WITH A BASKET OF FRUIT... A FARMER... SENSEI WU...
SENSEI WU?!
YOU SHOULD HAVE KEPT GOING. THEN ONE BLOW FROM BEHIND WOULD HAVE ENDED THINGS.
SENSEI, WHAT'S HAPPENED TO YOU?
I'VE SEEN THE TRUTH-- AND THE TRUTH IS HARD AS STONE.
EVEN STONE CAN BE SHATTERED IF YOU HIT IT THE RIGHT WAY!

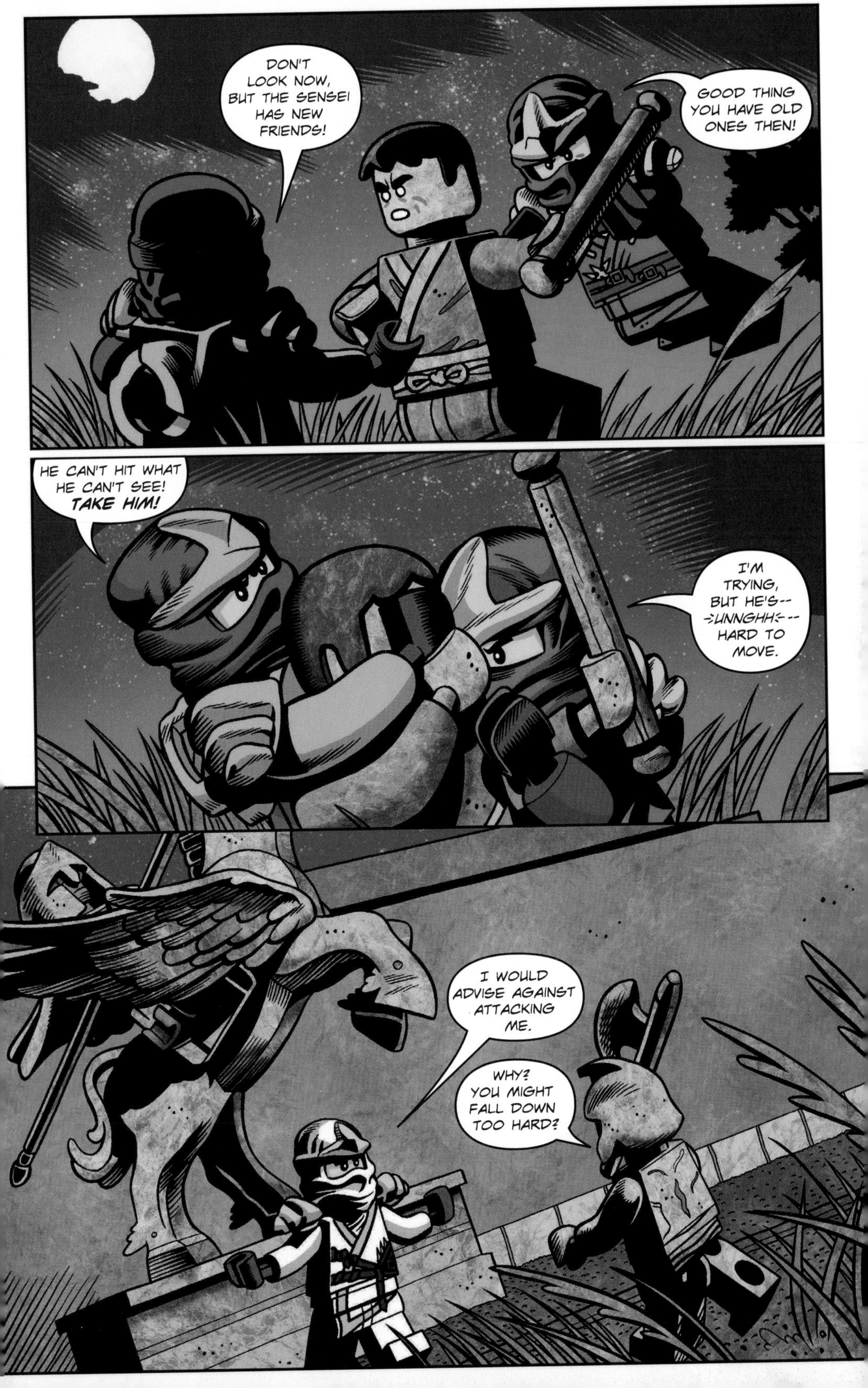
DON'T LOOK NOW, BUT THE SENSEI HAS NEW FRIENDS!
GOOD THING YOU HAVE OLD ONES THEN!
HE CAN'T HIT WHAT HE CAN'T SEE! **TAKE HIM!**
I'M TRYING, BUT HE'S-- -UNNGHH- -- HARD TO MOVE.
I WOULD ADVISE AGAINST ATTACKING ME.
WHY? YOU MIGHT FALL DOWN TOO HARD?

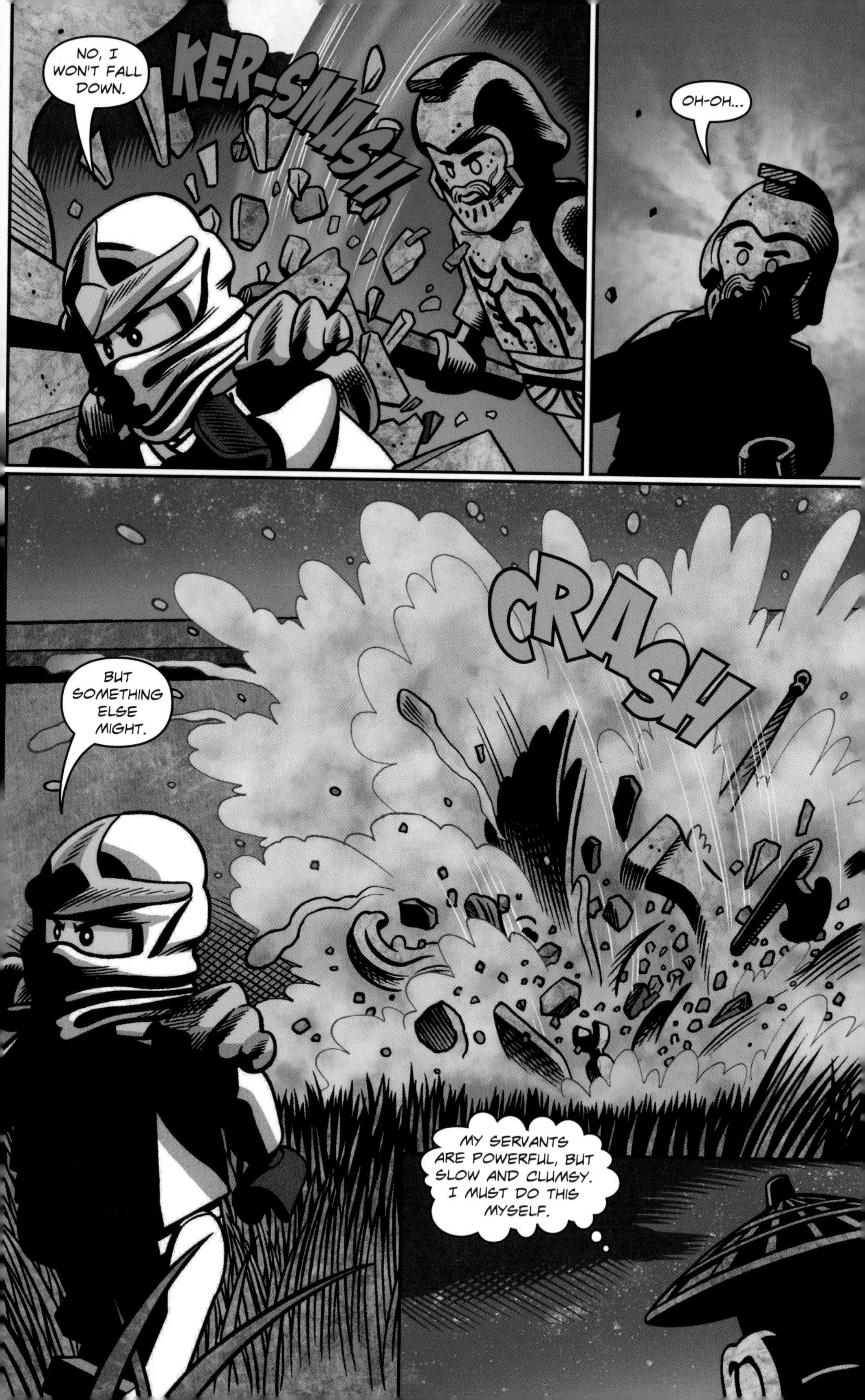
NO, I WON'T FALL DOWN.
KER-SMASH
OH-OH...
CRASH
BUT SOMETHING ELSE MIGHT.
MY SERVANTS ARE POWERFUL, BUT SLOW AND CLUMSY. I MUST DO THIS MYSELF.

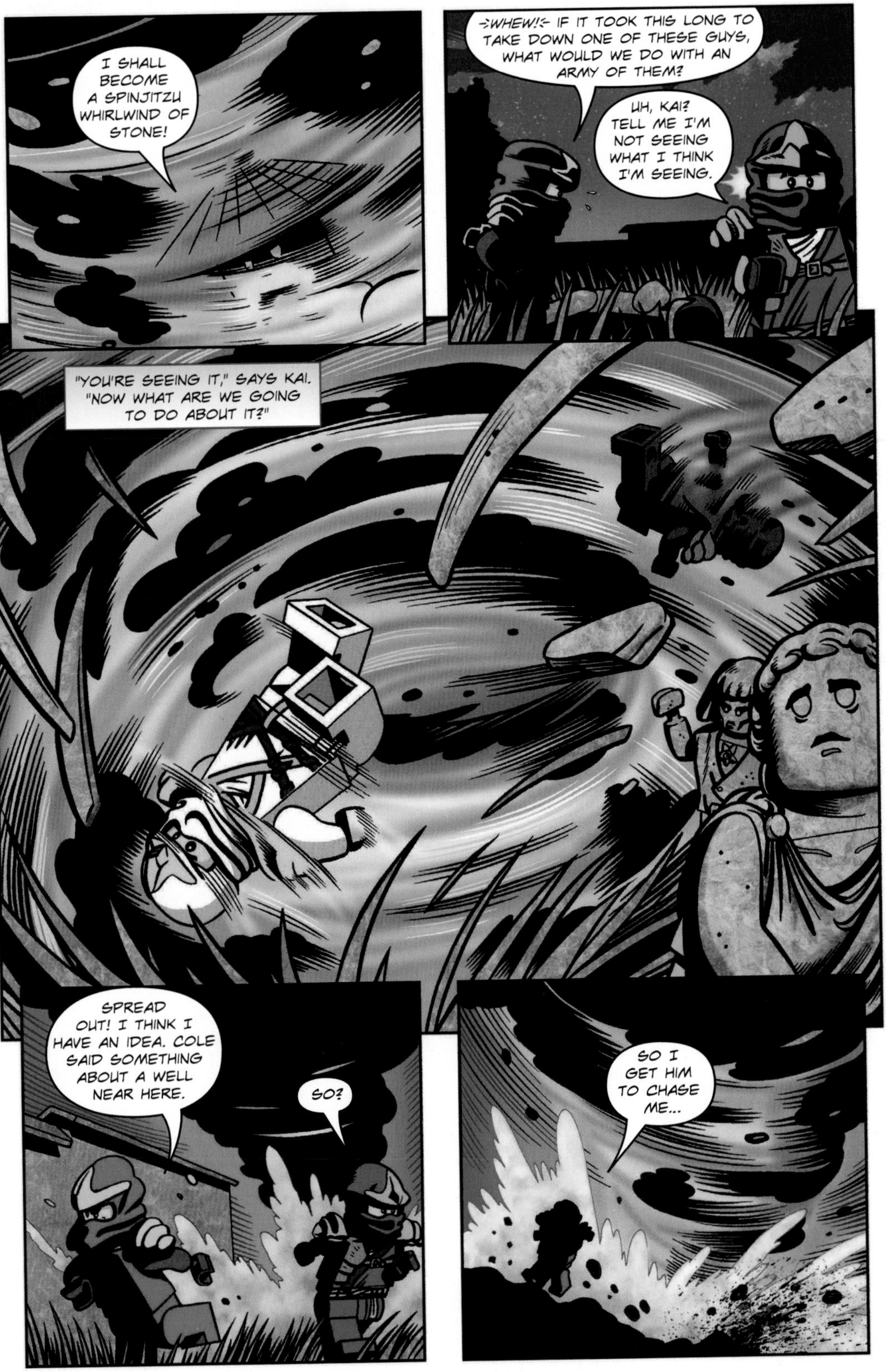
I SHALL BECOME A SPINJITZU WHIRLWIND OF STONE!
>WHEW!< IF IT TOOK THIS LONG TO TAKE DOWN ONE OF THESE GUYS, WHAT WOULD WE DO WITH AN ARMY OF THEM?
UH, KAI? TELL ME I'M NOT SEEING WHAT I THINK I'M SEEING.
"YOU'RE SEEING IT," SAYS KAI. "NOW WHAT ARE WE GOING TO DO ABOUT IT?"
SPREAD OUT! I THINK I HAVE AN IDEA. COLE SAID SOMETHING ABOUT A WELL NEAR HERE.
SO?
SO I GET HIM TO CHASE ME...

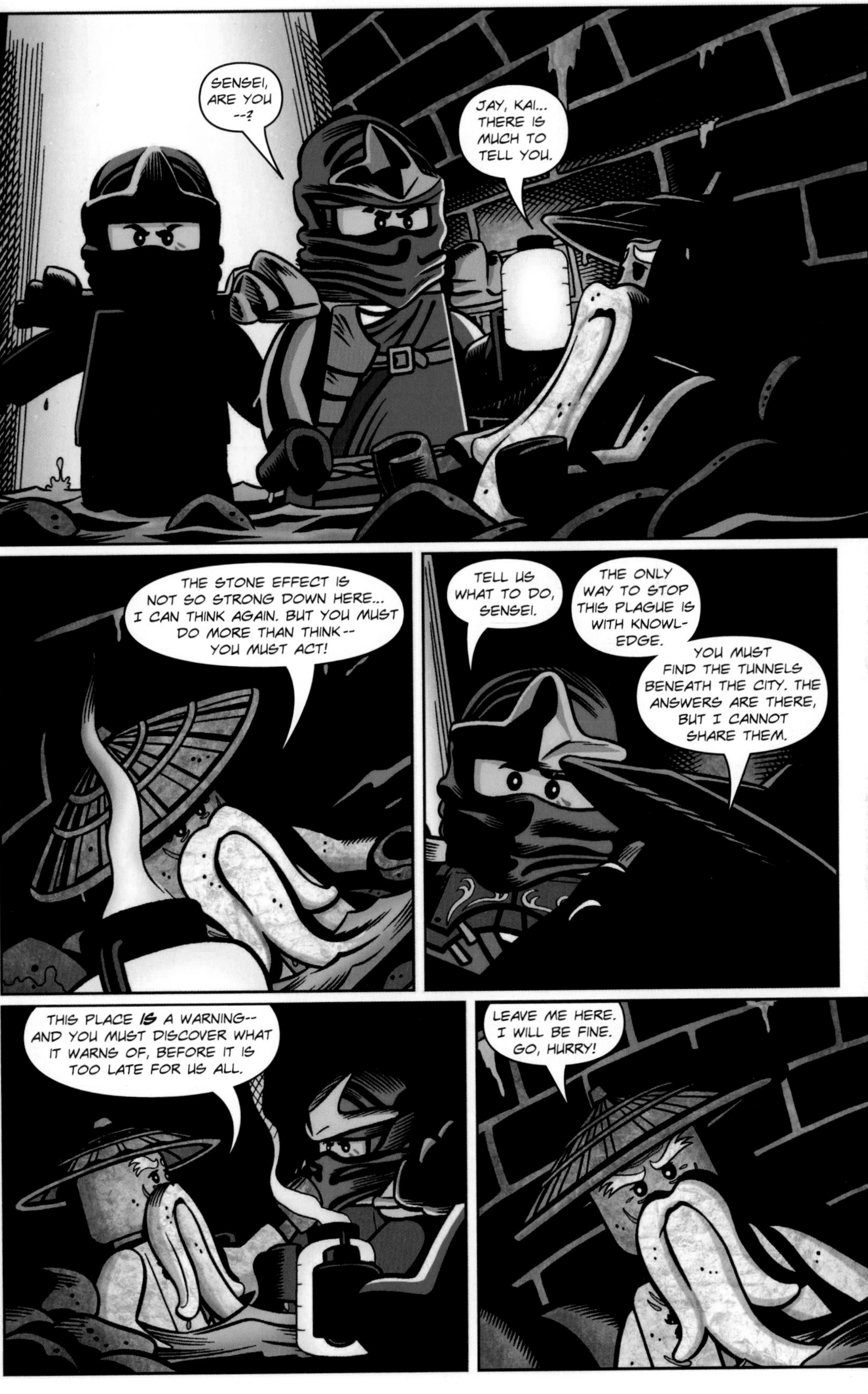
SENSEI, ARE YOU --?
JAY, KAI... THERE IS MUCH TO TELL YOU.
THE STONE EFFECT IS NOT SO STRONG DOWN HERE... I CAN THINK AGAIN. BUT YOU MUST DO MORE THAN THINK-- YOU MUST ACT!
TELL US WHAT TO DO, SENSEI.
THE ONLY WAY TO STOP THIS PLAGUE IS WITH KNOWL-EDGE.
YOU MUST FIND THE TUNNELS BENEATH THE CITY. THE ANSWERS ARE THERE, BUT I CANNOT SHARE THEM.
THIS PLACE IS A WARNING-- AND YOU MUST DISCOVER WHAT IT WARNS OF, BEFORE IT IS TOO LATE FOR US ALL.
LEAVE ME HERE. I WILL BE FINE. GO, HURRY!

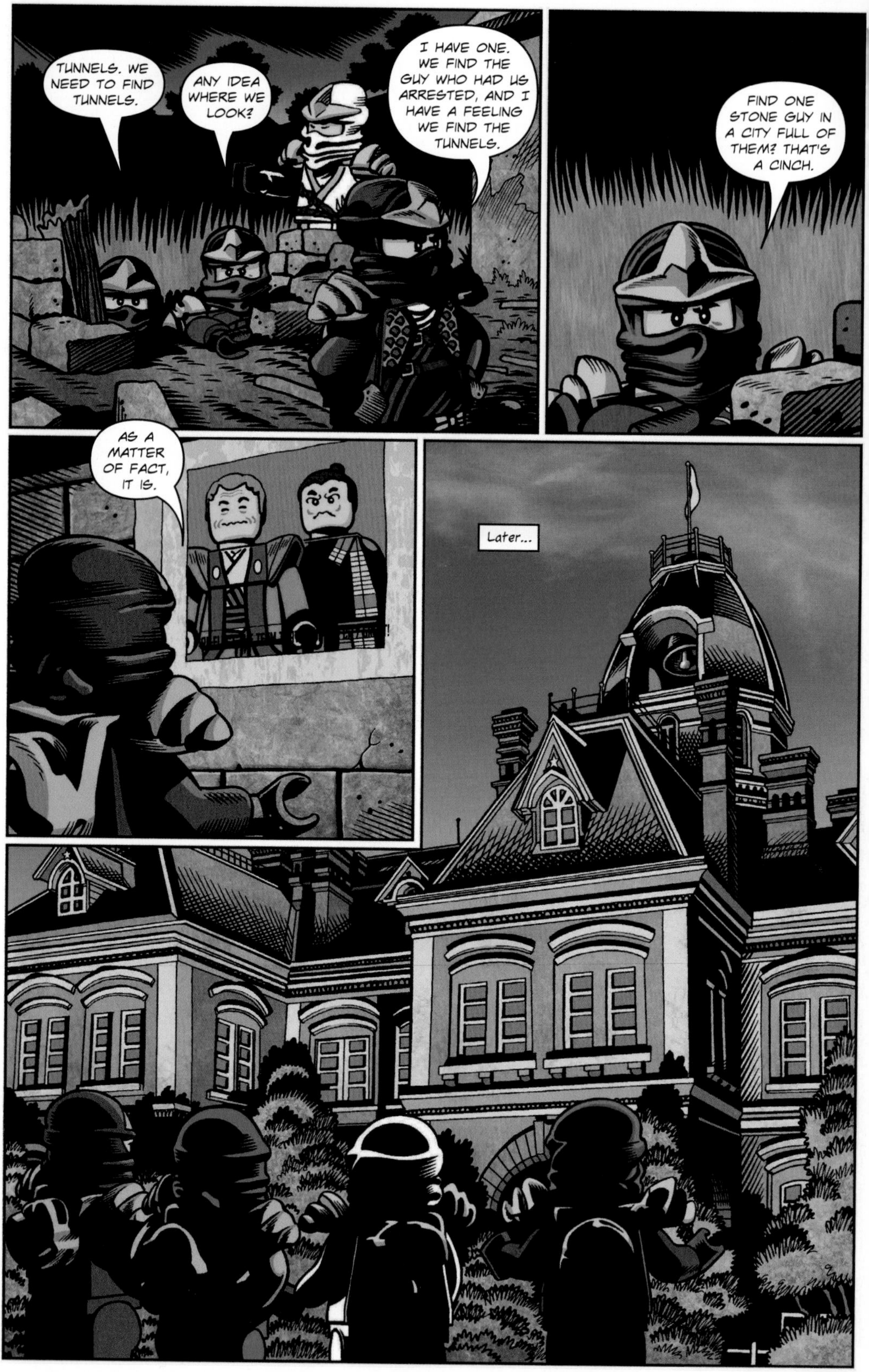
TUNNELS. WE NEED TO FIND TUNNELS.
ANY IDEA WHERE WE LOOK?
I HAVE ONE. WE FIND THE GUY WHO HAD US ARRESTED, AND I HAVE A FEELING WE FIND THE TUNNELS.
FIND ONE STONE GUY IN A CITY FULL OF THEM? THAT'S A CINCH.
AS A MATTER OF FACT, IT IS.
Later...

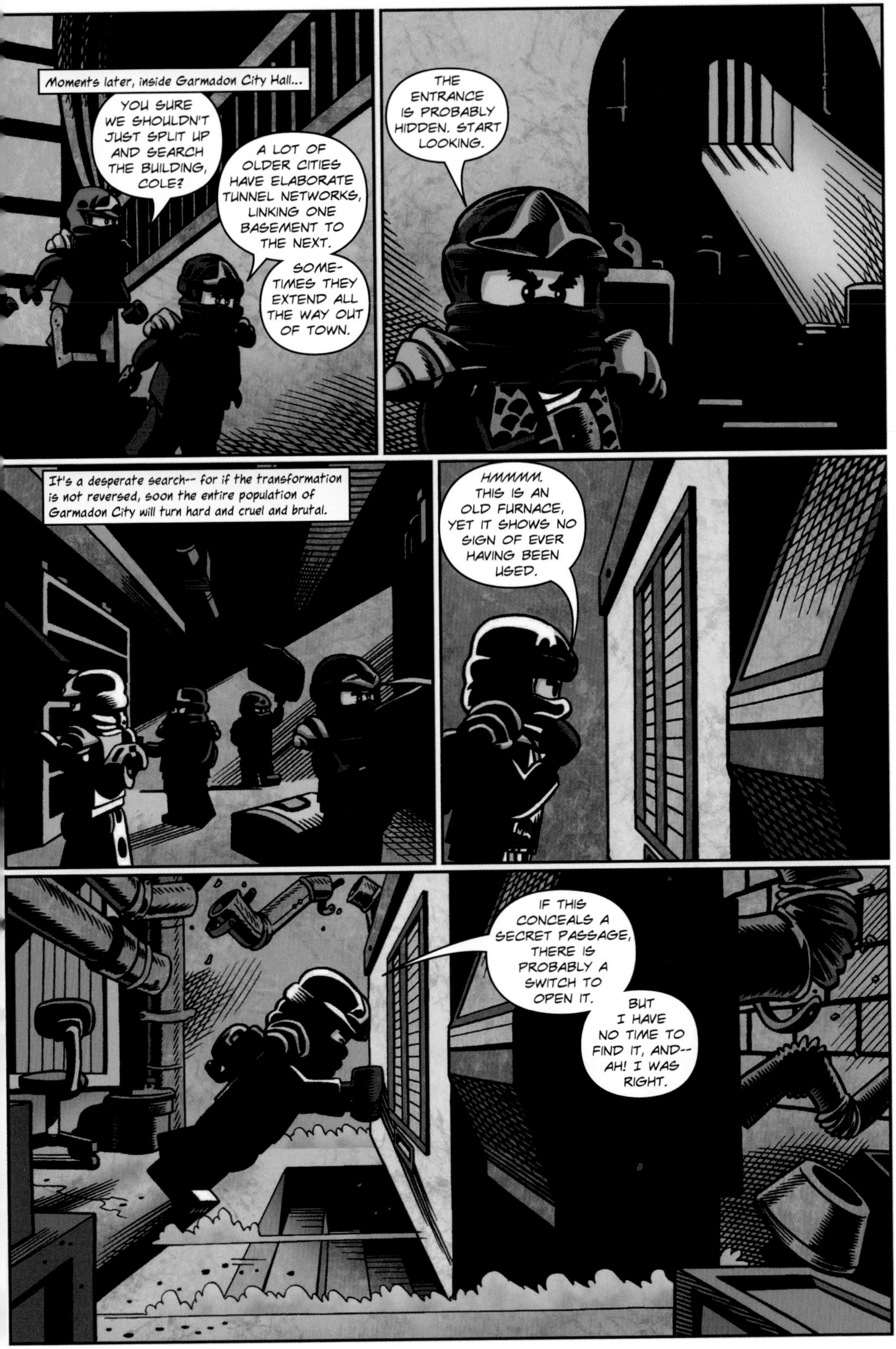
Moments later, inside Garmadon City Hall...
YOU SURE WE SHOULDN'T JUST SPLIT UP AND SEARCH THE BUILDING, COLE?
A LOT OF OLDER CITIES HAVE ELABORATE TUNNEL NETWORKS, LINKING ONE BASEMENT TO THE NEXT.
SOME-TIMES THEY EXTEND ALL THE WAY OUT OF TOWN.
THE ENTRANCE IS PROBABLY HIDDEN. START LOOKING.
It's a desperate search-- for if the transformation is not reversed, soon the entire population of Garmadon City will turn hard and cruel and brutal.
HMMMM. THIS IS AN OLD FURNACE, YET IT SHOWS NO SIGN OF EVER HAVING BEEN USED.
IF THIS CONCEALS A SECRET PASSAGE, THERE IS PROBABLY A SWITCH TO OPEN IT.
BUT I HAVE NO TIME TO FIND IT, AND-- AH! I WAS RIGHT.

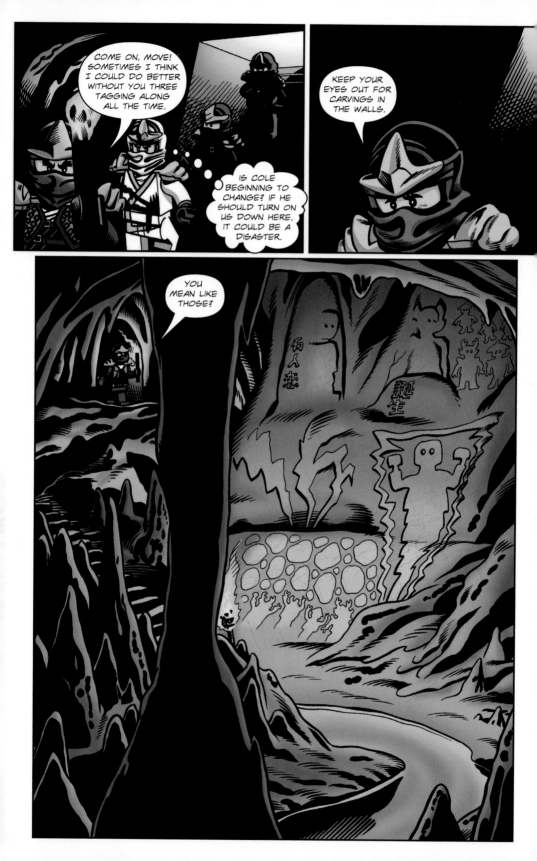

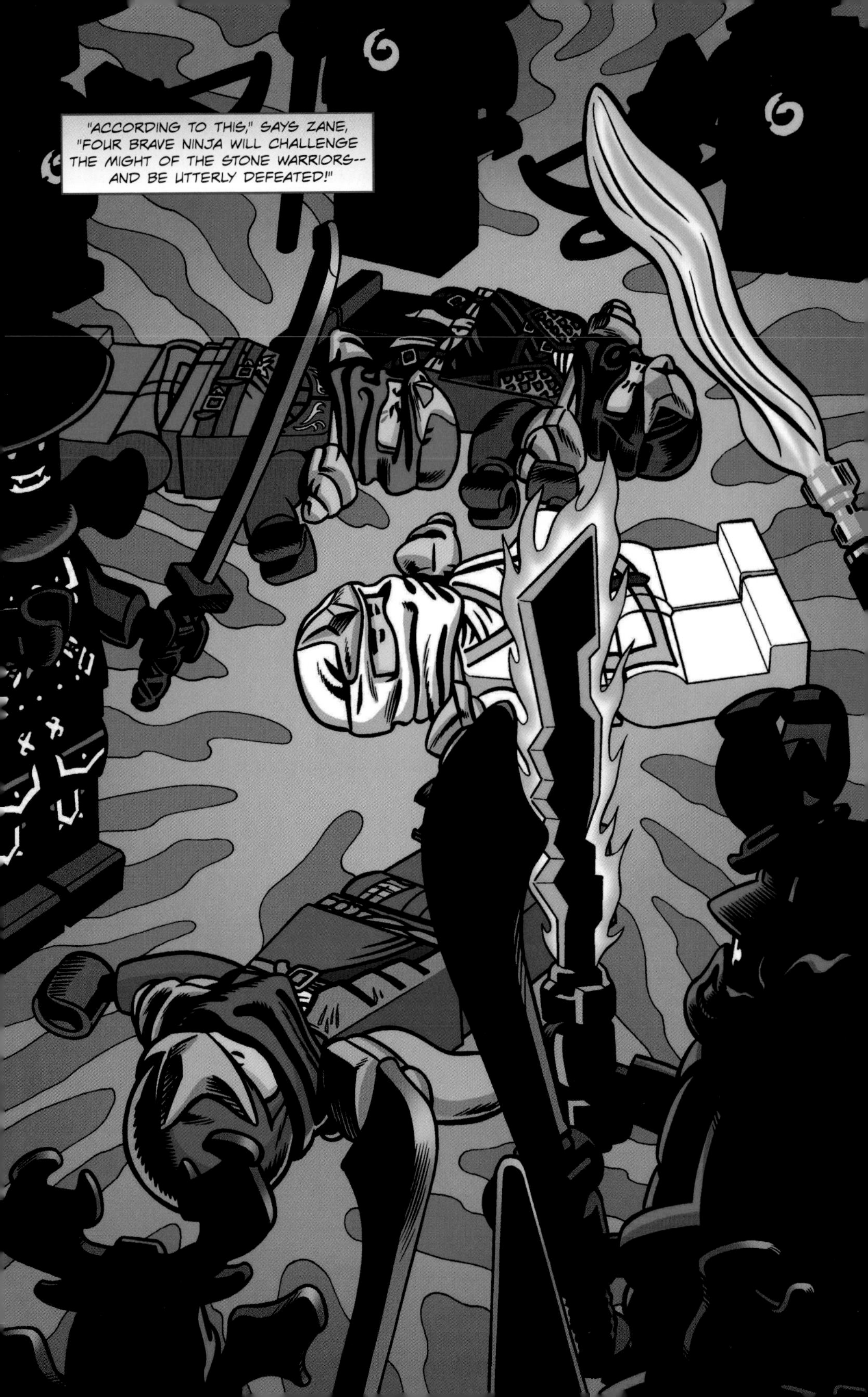
"ACCORDING TO THIS," SAYS ZANE, "FOUR BRAVE NINJA WILL CHALLENGE THE MIGHT OF THE STONE WARRIORS-- AND BE UTTERLY DEFEATED!"

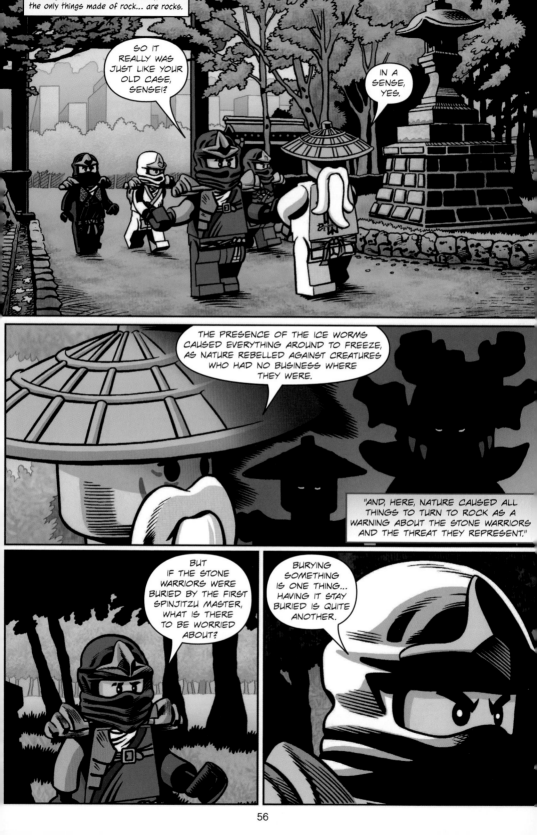

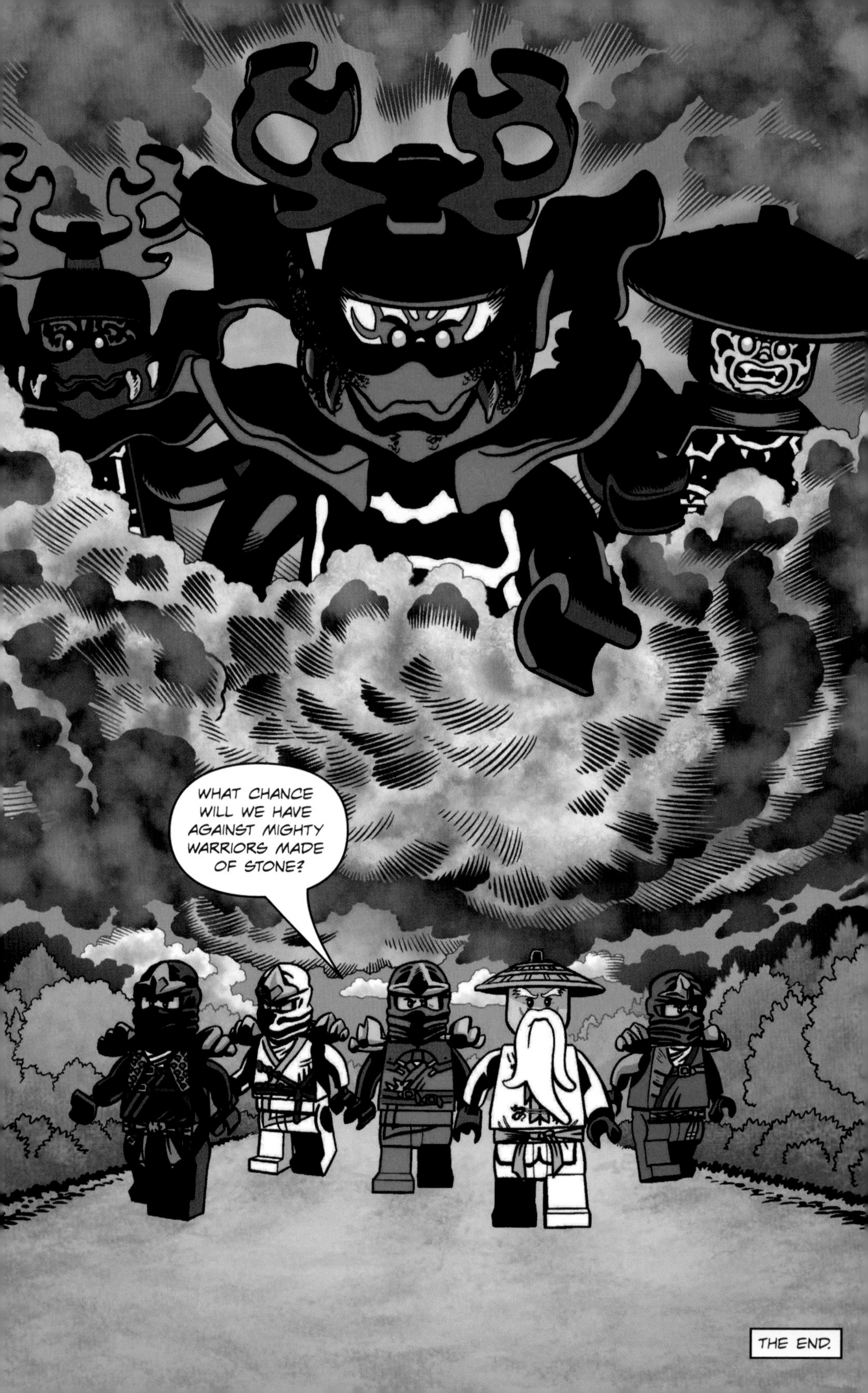
WHAT CHANCE WILL WE HAVE AGAINST MIGHTY WARRIORS MADE OF STONE?
THE END.

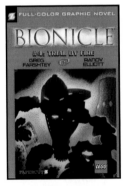

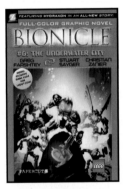

WATCH OUT FOR PAPERCUTZ™

Welcome to the virtually snake-less sixth LEGO® NINJAGO graphic novel from Papercutz, the little company dedicated to publishing great graphic novels for all ages. Of course, that's easy to do when working with such talented folks as writer Greg Farshtey, artist Jolyon Yates, colorist Jayjay Jackson, letterer Bryan Senka, and Associate Editor Michael Petranek. Don't tell Papercutz publisher Terry Nantier that with such an incredible creative crew, there's almost no need for me, Editor-in-Chief Jim Salicrup!

It seems that wherever you look these days, you're going to see NINJAGO! It's truly NINJAGO-MANIA! In addition to the best-selling Papercutz NINJAGO graphic novels, there's also the hit NINJAGO TV series on Cartoon Network and the NINJAGO chapter books from Scholastic. Perhaps the only place you don't find NINJAGO is on toy store shelves in the LEGO section—because they sell out so fast! (Don't give up, there's more on the way!)

Lest you think I may be exaggerating (who, me?), here's a story that'll set you straight. Recently, globe-trotting NINJAGO artist Jolyon Yates was out in the country in Australia, at the remotest restaurant he's ever been to-- and for some reason, he's been to a lot of remote restaurants! Fearlessly, he walks in and sees a boy named Owen:

Inside the restaurant, good ol' Jolyon was soon whipping up a sketch of Kai for the young NINJAGO fan. But the story doesn't end there! Then the chef rushes out of the kitchen to tell Jolyon that he just phoned his son in Brisbane, who's also a big NINJAGO fan! Of course, Jolyon was then drawing even more NINJAGO sketches! NINJAGO-MANIA is running wild!

Fortunately, you don't need to find Mr. Yates in the Land Down Under to get great artwork from him (I, mean that could get really expensive!). You simply need to go to your favorite bookseller or library soon and ask for LEGO NINJAGO #7 "Stone Cold"! Check out the sneak preview on the following pages...

So, until next time, keep spinnin'!

Thanks,

Jim

STAY IN TOUCH!

EMAIL: salicrup@papercutz.com
WEB: www.papercutz.com
TWITTER: @papercutzgn
FACEBOOK: PAPERCUTZGRAPHICNOVELS
FAN MAIL: Papercutz, 160 Broadway, Suite 700, East Wing, New York, NY 10038

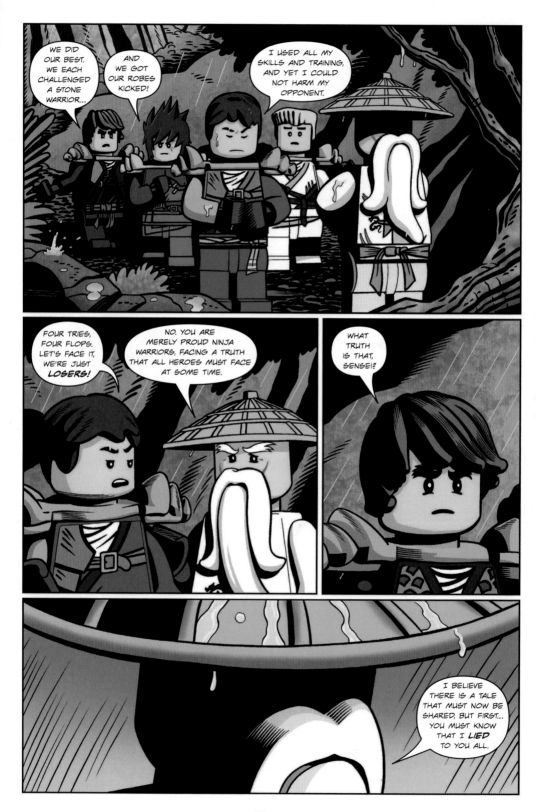

Don't Miss LEGO NINJAGO #7 "Stone Cold"!